MOONE BOY
The Fish Detective

Also available

Moone Boy: The Blunder Years

CHRIS O'DOWD
& NICK V. MURPHY

MOONE BOY

THE FISH DETECTIVE

ILLUSTRATED BY
WALTER GIAMPAGLIA/CARTOON SALOON

MACMILLAN CHILDREN'S BOOKS

First published 2015 by Macmillan Children's Books

This edition published 2016 by Macmillan Children's Books
an imprint of Pan Macmillan
20 New Wharf Road, London N1 9RR
Associated companies throughout the world
www.panmacmillan.com

ISBN 978-1-4472-7098-0 (PB)
ISBN 978-1-5098-3480-8 (IRISH EDITION)

Text copyright © Chris O'Dowd and Nick V. Murphy 2015
Illustrations copyright © Walter Giampaglia/Cartoon Saloon 2015

With thanks to Sky, Baby Cow Productions and Sprout Pictures

A CIP catalogue record for this book is available from
the British Library.

Printed and bound by CPI Group (UK) Ltd, Croydon CR0 4YY

To all the glorious migrants of the world – enjoy this book. But please don't use it as an example of good English. And to my son, Art, who emigrated from the womb around Chapter 6 and is already making a name for himself.

Chris

To my son, Jules, who showed up around Chapter 12. I hope this book is pleasant to chew on, is absorbent of your puke and will some day make you giggle as much as having a raspberry blown on your armpits.

Nick

Hello!

Sean 'Caution' Murphy here. Professional Imaginary Friend and Local Man of Mystery! (Apart from my name and occupation, which I just told you.)

Before we begin, please just check to make sure you're in the right book.

This is *Moone Boy: The Fish Detective*. If you've come for *Moo Joy: The Cow's Objective*, then you're in the wrong place – try the Nature section. Likewise, if you're looking for *Mean Boys: A Bully's Perspective*, *Food Toys: The Fun Congestive* or *Flu Boy: The Snotty Infective*, then please move along and ask for assistance.

But if you're in the *right* place, then welcome to this book! I'll be your book host! So come on in and make yourself at home. Put your feet up.

Not on the book though. Unless you don't mind reading through your toes.

Help yourself to some snacks – if you've brought some snacks. Snacks are not included with this book. Although you're very welcome to chew on the cover. All the red bits taste like strawberries.

OK, you ready? Then let's get this party started! Buckle up, slouch down and put your eyes to work, because these pages aren't going to read themselves! Unless you've bought the expensive Self-Reading Edition. In which case, press 'Auto-Read' now and enjoy a nice nap.

But the rest of you cheapskates – commence Manual Reading!

Signed,
Sean Murphy

PS I've just been informed that the red bits *don't* taste like strawberries. This is due to a malfunction by the printing machine. It seems that your new phonebook will taste like strawberries instead, and this book just tastes like a phonebook. But if you happen to like the finger-lickin' flavour of names and numbers, then lap it up, my friends, because you're in for a tasty treat!

CHAPTER ONE
FIFTY SLEEPS TO CHRISTMAS

A year is a very long time when you're an idiot.

When you think about it, there are very few things you could do for a whole year. You couldn't spend a year growing your toenails, for example, or you'd require some kind of hacksaw to trim them. You couldn't eat nothing but honey for an entire year, or bees would start growing in your belly. That's a fact – I looked it up. And you should avoid whistling the same song every day for a year or your classmates will eventually turn on you and staple your shoes to the ceiling – possibly while you're still wearing them, depending on the song.

To cope with the curse of the calendar, Martin Moone had developed the habit of dividing each year into smaller sections of roughly fifty days. Give or take a week here and there. These year sections, or 'yections' as he liked to call them, helped Martin cope with the vastness of time before him. He even named these yections, as a way of remembering them.

Boxing for Love: St Stephen's Day to Valentine's Day
Lovefool: Valentine's to April Fool's Day
Fool's Gold: April Fool's to 20th May (my
　　birthday, when I always ask for gold gifts)
Golden Days: 20th May to end of term!
Days of Wonder: summer holidays!
**Wonder what happened to the New School
　　Year:** start of term to 5th November
Why won't it end?: 5th November to Christmas
　　Day

The yection which always seemed to take the longest to pass was from 5th November to Christmas Day. The evenings were long, the rain was extra chilly and there were no birthdays to distract Martin. (It was actually his sister Sinead's birthday on 18th November, but every year one of the things she asked for was that Martin got none of her birthday cake – that was one of her actual presents, that Martin got no cake! – so he did his best to ignore her celebrations altogether.)

It was Sunday 5th November in the Moone home, and Martin and I decided to check his yection schedule to see what was in store for the fifty days ahead.

MON	TUE	WEN	THU	FRY	SAT	SUN
1	2	3 GEOGRAPHY TEST	4	5	6	7
8 DENTIST	9	10	11	12 GARBAGE COLLECTION	13	14
15	16	17	18 OPERATION STEAL SOME CAKE	19	20	21
22 SECOND DENTIST APPOINTMENT IF I FEEL FAINT THE FIRST TIME	23	24	25	26	27	28
29	30 RE-TAKE GEOGRAPHY TEST					

NOVEMBER

'Hmmm. Not much to get us excited there, buddy,' I grumbled.

But the one upside to entering the saddest yection in his made-up calendar was that it was now only FIFTY SLEEPS TO CHRISTMAS. You probably already knew that because you're a maths genius. And, also, this chapter is called 'Fifty Sleeps to Christmas'. But that had only just occurred to Martin, so he leaped to his feet and rushed into the kitchen to inform his mother. He knew it was unlikely she was aware of the significance of the day because her maths was pretty terrible and she probably hadn't yet read this book.

'Great news, Mam!' the boy blurted. 'It's only fifty sleeps till Christmas!'

'Did we not just have Christmas?'

'What?! No, silly,' he chuckled.

'That was over six yections ago!' I told her. Not that Martin's family could actually see me or hear me, but I liked shouting stuff at them anyway. 'Keep up, Moones!' I yelled.

'Anyway, not to put the pressure on,' Martin continued, 'but I was wondering how your Christmas-present-buying was going?'

Debra paused, which was a bit worrying, and glanced at Martin's dad, who was buttering some toast.

'Ahm, good, yeah,' Liam lied. 'We're torn between getting you new school trousers or fixing the sink in the bathroom. You love that sink, don't you?'

'You're funny, Dad!'

Liam and Debra shared a look that suggested they hadn't been joking at all.

Over the years, Martin had learned to keep expectations low around Christmas. He'd learned this by initially having extraordinarily high expectations (motorboat, diamond-encrusted tennis shoes, volcano holiday, etc.) and always ending up slightly disappointed (boat motor, new slippers, lava lamp, etc.).

'Give 'em the pitch, buddy,' I urged.

Martin nodded and laid out his demands to

his parents. 'I've put a lot of thought into this, folks, and after weeks of having my mind set on some kind of flying carpet for Christmas, my mind is now set on a Game Boy!'

'Your mind seems to set quite quickly,' Debra noted.

'Well, before it was only set like jelly, but now it's set like cement.'

'Who or what is a Game Boy?' Liam asked.

'It's a magical thing, Dad! It's like having a whole games arcade* in the palm of your hand!'

'Are these Game Boyos given out for free somewhere, by any chance?'

'Very funny, Dad. I can't imagine they cost less than a small fortune, but they're so worth it. Trevor at school has one and sometimes he lets me watch him playing it. It's really exciting. I can't even imagine how exciting it would be to *actually* play it.'

*GAMES ARCADE — a massive room containing games, toys and shady characters. This room was later replaced by the internet. MOONE DICTIONARY

'The thing is, Martin, money's a bit tight at the moment,' Liam said.

'Is it because Mam spends so much on vegetables? Because I've already offered a solution to that.'

'We can't just send all the vegetables to hell, Martin,' Debra sighed, as if this was a regular argument.

I checked out the dinner Debra was preparing and it actually looked like most of it had come from hell already, so her point was valid.

'Martin,' I said tentatively, 'I have some bad news about dinner.'

Martin peeked into the oven hoping to see his favourite Friday meal – pork shoulder, sausages and meat waffles. What he saw was disappointing.

'Are we having flippin' fish again?' he complained. 'We're not sharks, ya know!'

'Imagine if we *were* sharks though, buddy – living with a creature from the deep with razor-sharp teeth, the personality of a dead-eyed demon and jaws that could rip you apart!'

Just then Martin's sister Sinead entered the kitchen and we realized we already knew what that was like.

'If that bathroom sink leaks on me again, I'm gonna destroy it with my bare hands!' she said, scowling.

'Or your flippers!' I quipped.

Martin's ~~shark~~ sister leaned down to look through the oven window, dead-eyed.

'Are we having flippin' fish again?!' she grunted through her gills.

'C'mon now, Sinead,' Liam sighed. 'We all agreed at the family meeting* that we need to tighten our money belts for a while. So that means

*FAMILY MEETING — a weekly get-together arranged to shout at fellow family members.

more cheap fish dinners, and no – I repeat, NO!
– casual destruction of bathroom hardware.'

As this debate looked set to get violent,
Martin and I skulked* away towards the safety
of the living-room couch.

'Ya know what, buddy,' I started, 'I think if
we really want that Game Boy, we might have to
buy it ourselves.'

'Well, Sean, I could see how the back-of-
the-couch account is looking. We haven't
withdrawn from it since I bought those magic
beans from Declan Mannion.'

'What a waste of money *that* was.'

'How were we to know they were just peas?'

'Bottom line is, buddy, if we want a Game
Boy, we can't just sit around relying on the
kindness of strangers.'

'Or my family, for that matter,' Martin added
glumly.

'No, there's only one person you can

SKULK — to quietly move out of sight.
Originated from when the Incredible Hulk,
renowned for his smelly bottom, would
drop a fart and amble away, ashamed.

really depend on, Martin.'

'You?' he asked.

'No, definitely not me. I meant you!'

'Me?'

'Yes – who loves you more than you?'

'I don't know. You?'

'No, definitely not me.'

'So I need to rely on my own kindness to myself?'

'Exactly! What we need is a regular wage,' I said, as I perched on the back of the couch in prime thinking pose. 'Then we can buy all the Game Boys we want! We need to get you a job!'

'Yes! I'm twelve years old for crying out loud! It's high time I got a proper job.'

'A real job. For a real man. Making real money. And if we've got enough left over, we can get Christmas presents for the rest of the family too!'

'Let's not go bananas, Sean.'

'You're right, let's buy you a Game Boy and let the family watch you play it.'

'Perfecto!'

CHAPTER TWO

'But *why* can't I be a bin man?' demanded
Martin. 'I was born to be a bin man!'

A burly, bearded bin man lifted a sloppy sack
from the kerb and flung it into the garbage
truck. 'Well, for starters, you're not exactly a
"man", are ya?'

Martin looked insulted. 'What are you – some
kind of boy-bigot? You can't reject me just cos
I'm not a man!'

'Well, it's in the job title,' grunted beardy
with a shrug, as he climbed on to the back of
the trash truck. 'Bin *man*,' he stated, pointing at
himself. 'No one needs a bin *boy*,' he scoffed.

The truck moved off and Martin chased after
it. 'Aw, come on, mister! No one knows rubbish
better than me! I love rubbish! Our house is full

sh dump!'

...er and

...stration.

...ow much

...

...him, 'we'll find

...-man boy-bigot

is right. ... should stop going for jobs that have "man" in the title.'

Martin nodded glumly, 'Well, since I've been rejected as a barman, a bin man and a stuntman, we're running out of man-jobs all right.' He furrowed his brow, thinking. 'So, what jobs have "boy" in the title?'

We pondered this as we ambled back down Main Street towards the heart of the town.

'Stable boy?' I suggested.

'Aren't I allergic to horses?'

'Good point. How about cowboy?'

'Same problem really.'

'Schoolboy?'

'I think I'm already a schoolboy.'

'Does it pay well?'

'Not really.'

'Game Boy!'

'I don't think that's a job.'

'No, but it's what we're after. Just trying to keep us focused here, Martin.'

'Good thinking,' he said with a nod. Then suddenly he had a thought. 'Hey, remember that weird song that Trevor was rapping at us the other day?'

Martin's classmate Trevor had developed a fondness for rapping ever since he'd acquired his rap-loving imaginary friend, Loopy Lou. The awfulness of their 'rap attacks' was difficult to forget.

'You mean, about being "a homeboy"?' I asked.

'That's the one! Maybe I could be a homeboy!'

'A homeboy! Brilliant!' I cried. 'What is it?'

'Someone . . . who likes being at home?' he guessed.

'That's perfect!' I exclaimed. 'You were born to be a homeboy!'

We high-fived each other happily, then stood there for a moment, thinking.

'Although . . .' I ventured, 'are we absolutely sure that's a real job? Trevor's rapping has led us astray before. Remember that time he told you to "Pump Up the Volume" and you stuck that bicycle pump into the radio and nearly electrocuted yourself?'

Martin shook his head ruefully. 'That was a really confusing thing to say.'

'*Really* confusing,' I agreed. 'No one should rap in riddles when electrics are involved.'

Just then, Martin noticed something across the street. 'What's that?' he squeaked excitedly, peering through my stomach. He could do this sometimes if he squinted his eyes just right and remembered that I wasn't actually there.

'What's what?'

But he was already scampering across the road. He raced over to a sign that hung in the window of 'News for Youse*', a little newsagent shop on the corner.

Martin read the sign with growing excitement. 'Wanted. Paperboy!' he exclaimed.

*YOUSE — the plural of 'you', pronounced 'yooze'. Irish pronouns are organized like this: Us, them, you, yer man, yer wan, ye, youse, you lot, them lot, the lot of them, what's-his-name, what's-her-face, the fella over there, that shower of chancers behind the gate.

'Wow,' I marvelled. 'A Wanted poster – like in the Wild West. Is there a reward for this paperboy?'

'What? No, I think it's a job.'

'A job! Even better! And it's got "boy" in the title!'

Martin grinned and straightened his woolly hat. 'Looks like everything's finally coming up Moone.'

He thrust open the door and marched into the shop.

'Hello, good shopkeep! I'm here for the plum post of paperboy.'

A short, round man was slouched behind the counter, slowly restocking a lollipop display. He regarded Martin with mild suspicion.

'Any experience?' he asked in a dull drone.

'No. But I think I'm more than qualified.'

'Why's that?'

'Well, er . . . do I need any qualifications?'

'No.'

'Then I'm more than qualified! Here's my CV*!' announced Martin, and slapped it down proudly on the counter.

*CV — a list of stuff you've done. Stands for 'Curriculum Vitae' in Latin, or 'Creative Vomit' in English, as it's usually an inventive mess of lies and half-chewed-truths.

C V

MARTIN PAUL KENNY DALGLISH MOONE

'A GRAND LITTLE FELLA' - GRANDAD.

'A HAPPY ACCIDENT' - MAM.

'TWO THUMBS UP' - PADRAIC O'DWYER.

CURRENT POSITION:

          LOYAL SON AND FUTURE HEIR TO THE MOONE ESTATE.

PREVIOUS POSITION:

          EXPLORER.
          ARCHITECT.
          INVENTOR OF THE 'MIX TAPE'.
          (A BLEND OF SELLOTAPE AND DUCT TAPE).

SPECIAL SKILLS:

          C V WRITING.
          SPULLING.
          SPEED-EATING SPAGHETTI.
          RESTING.

The shopkeeper looked up from the CV, weirdly unimpressed.

'Tell ya what,' he said at last, and handed a newspaper to Martin, 'Take this paper and let's see if you can push it through that letter box.'

Martin saluted. 'I'm on it, sir!'

He snatched the paper and ran outside. Then he stuffed it through the letter box as fast as he could. When it dropped to the floor, he barged back into the shop. 'How'd I do?' he asked eagerly.

'You're hired.'

'Yes!' exclaimed Martin, and punched the air.

'Be here at 6 a.m. to collect the papers.'

'6 a.m.?!'

'Oh balls,' I murmured. 'I knew this was too good to be true. Next he'll probably tell us that our delivery motorbike doesn't even have a sidecar.'

'Is 6 a.m. a problem?' the man enquired.

'It's just, er . . . I'm not a big "morning person",' Martin confessed. 'I struggle with mornings, truth be told. I'm cursed with a terrible fondness for sleep.'

'You want the job, don't ya?'

'Oh very much so, sir!' replied Martin. 'But perhaps I could deliver the papers a bit later in the day. Maybe in the afternoon?'

'About 4 p.m. would be perfect,' I suggested, consulting our diary.

The shopkeeper frowned at Martin. 'But people like their paper in the morning.'

'Yes, but we could be different!' Martin countered. 'We could be the afternoon newspaper!'

'But . . . it'd still be the same paper. Just delivered late.'

'Or early!' replied Martin confusingly. 'Cos if you think about it, the afternoon is actually earlier than the morning.'

'How do you mean?'

'Well, right now is earlier than tomorrow, isn't it?'

The shopkeeper was struggling to keep up

with Martin's logic. 'But delivering it now would only be earlier if you had tomorrow's paper.'

'Even better! I'll deliver tomorrow's paper! Today!'

'But I just have today's paper.'

'Then get me tomorrow's paper! And I'll deliver it every day, some time in the late afternoon, probably between four and six-ish – sharp! Do we have ourselves a deal, sir?' asked Martin enthusiastically.

'You're fired,' droned the shopkeeper, and went back to his lollipops.

CHAPTER THREE
CROSS COUNTRY MEATS

'I hear ya, Martin. Finding decent work is tricky in this day and age.'

Martin was filling in his best friend, Padraic, on his job-hunting woes. He often looked to his pal for advice on these matters because Padraic was wise beyond his years. Also, nobody else wanted to listen to Martin's boring problems. It was break time, so the boys were walking through the school playground, avoiding various calls and balls whizzing past their dopey heads as Padraic pondered Martin's career complaints.

'I blame Wall Street,' Padraic said wisely.

'Wall Street, P-Dog?'

'Yeah, it's that road just outside Boyle that has a bunch of different wall-building companies on it.'

'Oh yeah,' Martin remembered.

'The local job market has been a nightmare since walls went out of fashion.'

'Yeah, it's all fences and hedges these days,' Martin agreed.

'To be fair, they are a lot cheaper.'

'Yeah, even Dad's got a hedge fund going now.'

'Where could you work?' Padraic asked himself, rubbing his pudgy chin. 'Who could use a Martin Moone around? It's a tricky one, Martin. I'm afraid I'm fresh out of ideas at the mo-OWW!'

A large marble had just flown past Martin's head and smacked into Padraic's temple* with a dull thud.

*TEMPLE — a part of the human head, halfway between the top of your ear and the bottom of your eyebrow. It's called the 'temple' as it's where hair nits go to pray.

Luckily the clatter to the cranium seemed to wake up Padraic's thinking jelly and he raised his finger in triumph. 'Hey! Maybe I could get you some part-time work in my family butcher shop?'

'Your family owns a butcher shop?'

'Only the finest meats and poultry in Boyle, Right Beside Boyle and Just Outside Boyle!'

'But . . . I thought your family were farmers?'

'Well, my dad is a farmer, but his six brothers run an abattoir* and my Auntie Bridget runs the Cross Country Meats butcher shop on Grub Street.'

'Wow, your family has really cornered the meat market.'

'Yeah, we like to think of ourselves as a cradle-to-grave dinner service.'

*ABATTOIR — this is like a boudoir** for animals. They go to sleep there. (But they never wake up.)

**BOUDOIR — a type of bedroom in France where, historically, magic has happened.

'Ya really think your auntie would give me a job?' Martin asked eagerly.

'Well . . . Let's see – do you have any meat retail experience?'

'None.'

'Are you a hard worker?'

'Not really.'

'Do you steal?'

'Rarely.'

'Are you punctual?'

'Never.'

'Can you lie about all that?'

'Absolutely!'

'Then I don't see why not. I'll set up an interview!'

After school that day, Padraic took Martin to meet the meat queen. But on their way through town, Martin started to get nervous about the impending interview with Bridget Cross. Nerves always gave him a dry mouth. To counteract this, he had chugged down three cans of Lilt*, two glasses of Milt** and a carton of Kilt*** by the time they hit Grub Street.

*LILT — a popular fizzy drink with a totally tropical taste.
**MILT — a slightly less popular fizzy drink with a totally dairy taste.
***KILT — an extremely unpopular fizzy drink with a totally Scottish taste.

'So tell me about your Auntie Bridget, P-Dog. How do I make a good impression? Should I use my boyish charm or my macho manly moves? I'm equally mediocre at both.'

'Hmm. She's a tough nut, Martin. She was the only girl in a family with seven bawdy brothers. Then she got married to an eejit called Christian Cross, who ran off with a South American choral singer he met at their wedding.'

'So . . .' Martin asked tentatively, 'go easy on being male at all, maybe?'

'I'll tell ya what, Martin – she loves talking in Irish. She's old school like that. If you can speak Irish, you'll be nailed on for the job. How's your Irish?'

'Ahm . . . Thing is . . . Mr Jackson always teaches Irish right after lunch, which, as you know, is when I like to take my main school nap. So . . . long story short, I only really know one sentence in Irish.'

'O-kaaay. What is it?'

Martin cleared his throat, and said,

'*Múinteoir, an bhfuil cead agam dul go dtí an leithreas, le do thoil?*'

TRANSLATION

'Teacher, may I go to the toilet please?'

'That's the only Irish you know?'

'That's it, I'm afraid. After nap time and pee time, Irish class is usually over and we're into history class, or as I call it, fidget-and-doodle hour.'

'Right. Well, maybe try to keep the conversation in English,' Padraic suggested, with the tone of someone who could feel a failure coming.

Martin nodded glumly as they reached the front door of Cross Country Meats. A cowbell above the shop door clanged clunkily as they entered the butcher shop.

'Auntie Bridget?' Padraic called into the seemingly empty room.

Martin straightened his elastic tie as his eyes searched the shop for a living lady. He could see plenty of deceased creatures behind cold glass – turkey legs, minced meat, lamb balls – but nobody with a pulse. At a counter in the back he seemed to spot what could only be described as a floating hat.

'*As Gaeilge, a Phádraic, as Gaeilge!*'

TRANSLATION

'In Irish, Padraic, in Irish!'

Confused, Martin watched as the floating hat moved from behind the back counter and turned into a human woman.

Bridget Cross was a tiny little lady, barely taller than Martin. I'm not great at judging age, but if I had to guess, I'd say she was around a hundred and three. Though it's more likely she was about half that. Her cheeks were the colour of red roses that have been sitting in a vase a week too long. She wore her tangerine hair high in a bun beneath her butcher's hat. The height of the white cap made it look as if her hair was trying to carry her off into space or something. Every inch of her was covered in wool. She had a woolly cardigan and a moss-coloured woolly skirt which met tall woolly socks at the knee. She had slightly fluffy sideburns and a faint ginger moustache above her thin, cracked lips, so even her face was a little woolly. On her chest sat a bronze brooch, which sagged a bit because of its weight. When the sun caught it, light would beam from it and temporarily blind you if you stood too close. She was the most Irish person Martin had ever met.

'Pádraic, an séú nia is fearr liom, cén chaoi a bhfuil tú?'

'I'm grand, Auntie Bridget. This is Martin, who I called you about. He's a wonderful fella, and I think he'd make a brilliant—'

'Whisht*!' she spluttered.

We all fell silent.

She stared at Martin, taking him in. 'Let me have a look at you then.'

*WHISHT — the Irish equivalent of 'Shush', but a bit wetter, like most things Irish.

34

She was already looking at him, but seemed to expect more. Martin looked to me, slightly confused.

'I think . . . she wants you to do a little twirl, buddy,' I suggested.

Martin did a little twirl, like a toddler in a beauty pageant. As he finished his spin, he felt a rumble in his tummy. All the Lilt, Milt and Kilt from earlier had made their way to his bladder and were now eager to join the potty party. He desperately needed to wee. But Bridget Cross was still staring at him.

'Hmmmm,' she said, in Irish. Or any language I suppose.

'*Mairtín, sé an rud is tábhachtaí sa ghnó bia, ná glantanas. Má tá tú míghlan in aon chaoi ar bith, inis dom anois é.*'

Martin stared at her, completely clueless. All he could think of was his bursting bladder. His eyes narrowed as he looked blankly back at Bridget Cross, certain he was about to wet himself.

'Do something, Martin!' I shouted unhelpfully.

'*Múinteoir, an bhfuil cead agam dul go dtí an leithreas, le do thoil?*' he said hopefully.

Bridget seemed taken aback by his response.

'Of course, my boy!' she beamed as she pointed past the lamb counter to the toilet in the back.

Martin waddled off desperately, presuming he'd blown his chance of a job.

Bridget turned to Padraic. 'What a lovely young man. Good Irish, and the honesty to appreciate that his hands needed cleaning, and . . . he called me his teacher! I like that. I like when someone instantly realizes that there are many things they can learn from me.'

'I told you he was a wonderful fella, Auntie Bridget.'

'And I told you whisht!'

They stood in silence a moment as Bridget considered what to do with Martin.

'Fine,' she said at last. 'I'll take him on.'

And just like that, with a full bladder and an empty head, Martin Moone managed to get his first job. He was going to be a butcher boy!

CHAPTER FOUR
THE BUTCHER BOY

After the initial excitement of gaining
employment, Martin was disappointed to
discover that there was actually very little
for him to do in Cross Country Meats. He ran
there straight after school every day and
quickly donned his handy hairnet, stylish
butcher's cap and white coat, but after that
he mostly just stood around trying to make
the pigs' heads make funny faces or kiss each
other.

The butcher shop was strangely quiet.
Business was slow – much slower than usual –
and this was worrying Bridget Cross.

Christmas was fast approaching,
but they'd had hardly any orders for
turkeys. Ham sales were down too.

Only giblet* sales were steady. (They sold one bag of giblets every year, and Martin's teacher, Mr Jackson, had already placed his order.) But apart from this, meat numbers were down across the board.

*GIBLETS — foul-looking fowl guts.

Something was clearly not right, and Bridget Cross seemed to know exactly where to lay the blame for her meat misfortunes. Every day she stood at the window and glared across the street with contempt.

'That flippin' fish shop,' she growled.

Francie Feeley's Fabulous Fishatorium stood directly across the road from Cross Country Meats. The little shop was painted a bright salmon pink and decorated with colourful pictures of anchors, buoys and smiling shellfish. A large blue plastic dolphin was displayed proudly above the entrance – although, confusingly, dolphin was the one fish they didn't seem to sell. (Martin and I had discovered this one day after watching a TV show called *Flipper* about a crime-solving dolphin. We decided that a dolphin detective would make the perfect pet for us and could happily live in the bath. But – because apparently dolphins aren't actually fish! Who knew?! – the Fishatorium didn't sell dolphins, so all we got was a tin of sardines, whose ability to float was about as impressive as its ability to solve crimes.)

Under the plastic dolphin, there was a sea-blue door with a cockle-shaped doorbell, and on either side of this were two large round windows. These were home to the Fishatorium's famous window displays. Each week, fish would be arranged in a kind of 'diorama*', wearing little costumes and all carefully arranged to show a dramatic scene. For example, they did *The Last Fish Supper* – similar to the painting *The Last Supper* – except instead of Jesus and his disciples, this one had a bearded bass eating dinner with several sole, and an evil-looking piranha, which symbolized Judas. Other memorable ones were *Starfish Wars*, *Indiana Fishbones: Raiders of the Lost Carp*, and *Snow Whiting and the Seven Squids*.

*DIORAMA — this word can either mean 'a model of a scene with little figures standing inside it' or else 'the diarrhoea of a llama'. Just depends on the situation.

In contrast to the tumbleweed rolling
through Cross Country Meats, the Fishatorium
was always packed to the gills. It was only open
for a couple of hours every day, but that just
seemed to attract the customers even more,
and it did ten times more business in those
two hours than Bridget did all day. Customers
would line up outside, waiting, until finally the
doors would open and loud music would blare

out on to the street – songs like *Under the Sea*, *Gone Fishin'* and the theme music from *Jaws*. Every day there were great deals to be had, and Bridget just couldn't compete.

'All anybody wants these days is fish, fish, cheap flippin' fish,' she'd grumble.

But it wasn't simply that the Fishatorium kept its prices low. The fish were also so finely filleted. Not a bone in sight. And so fresh too! 'It's like eating a live fish!' the customers would say. 'Like taking a chomp out of the ocean!'

'*Conas a dhéatar é, Martín?!* How do they do it?!' yelled Bridget one day, both in Irish and English, as she was doubly furious.

Martin, who was in the middle of trying to build a sausage pyramid, jumped to attention. 'I dunno,' he replied, unsure what she was on about. 'Maybe they just *inject* the fig inside the roll?'

'I'm not talking about fig rolls, I'm talking about fish!' she snapped. 'Every day, crates and crates of them arrive from the factory –

but how? No one works up there, Martin. The factory hasn't been hiring for years. So who's doing it all? A family of elves? A load of fish-gutting robots?'

'Or maybe an army of trained monkeys!' I suggested excitedly.

'There's something fishy going on,' she muttered darkly, '*Rud éigin an-fishy go deimhin.*'

TRANSLATION
Something very fishy indeed.

Just then, the music across the street fell silent and a friendly-looking man with greasy hair strolled out of the shop, stuffing bundles of cash into his pockets.

'There he is now,' said Bridget hatefully.

'*Féach air, Martín.* Cock of the walk. Johnny come lately. Captain flippin' Birdseye.'

TRANSLATION
'Look at him, Martin.'

Martin watched the man locking up the shop, curious. He was dressed in green corduroy trousers, a woolly jumper with a picture of a fish on it and a brown tweed jacket. He also wore a glittering array of rings on his fingers and a shiny gold chain that dangled around his neck.

'Who is that handsome grease-ball?' he asked.

'Well,' I mused, 'based on his jewellery, I'd say he must be either a mayor, a gypsy king or some kind of fish-loving rapper.'

'Who is he?!' grunted Bridget, 'He's the fish king of Boyle, that's who. The Kingfisher himself, the Codfather of Sole: Francie 'Touchy' Feeley.'

Francie was waving goodbye to his customers, giving everyone lots of hugs and kisses.

'Now don't forget to order your Christmas fish, ladies!' he was telling them, pointing to a notice on the door. 'I'll have something very special for ye. Once you've had one of these beauties you'll never go near a miserable ol' turkey again!'

'Fish is the new turkey?' muttered Bridget. 'We'll see about that.'

FISH IS THE NEW TURKEY!
Order your Christmas Fish NOW and collect it right here on Christmas Eve. Only 5 pound! (Or 4 pound with a sloppy kiss! Hahaha. That's a genuine offer.)

Francie started to amble away, but then spotted Bridget peering at him through the window.

'Oh, hi, Bridget!' he called, with a big friendly wave.

'Hiya!' she called back, waving sweetly. But as he disappeared down the street, her face darkened again. 'I'll find out your secrets some day, Francie Feeley,' she whispered threateningly.

'Yeah,' chirped Martin. 'And when we do, we'll make *our own* fig rolls!'

'Why do you keep talking about fig rolls, you *amadán**?!' snapped Bridget.

He smiled and nodded cluelessly, pretending he understood the Irish word. '*Múinteoir, an*

***AMADÁN** — word number 79 for 'idiot'. This one's in Irish.

bhfuil cead agam dul go dtí an
leithreas, le do thoil?'

TRANSLATION

Teacher, may
I go to the
toilet please?

She frowned at him. 'Ya know, you've got a very weak bladder, Martin. I'd get that checked out if I were you.'

CHAPTER FIVE
FRANCIE 'TOUCHY' FEELEY

Francie 'Touchy' Feeley was a friendly man.
Very friendly. Fiercely friendly and terribly
touchy, I'd say. He got the nickname 'Touchy'
Feeley because he'd hug and kiss anyone he met
in the street, be they friend, foe or complete
stranger. This wouldn't have been a problem
had his profession not been so fish-scented.
How can I describe the dilemma? Well . . . ya
know your auntie who insists on kissing your
face every time she comes over? Well, imagine
if your auntie washed in a bath full of tuna
each morning. That's what Francie smelled
like. With the addition of bad teeth and a wispy
moustache. (Some aunties also have wispy
moustaches but you really shouldn't mention
those, and never, ever buy them shaving foam

for their birthday. Trust me on this.)

Despite living in Boyle for years, Francie had an air of mystery about him, and rumours followed behind him as closely as his unfortunate odour. He was thought to be from the west coast, the only son of a fisherman and a fisherwoman. Many said that he was even born in the hull of a fishing boat. Another rumour suggested that he was raised by dolphins on an island in the middle of the Atlantic Ocean and that he had gills on his back. But it was Padraic who started that rumour, so I'd take it with a pinch of salt.

It was to his credit that, despite these vicious rumours and his unpleasant aroma,

Francie Feeley had managed to create something of an aquatic empire. Intrigued by his story and bored by our own lives, Martin and I decided to delve into Francie's world of fish. So we headed to the hub of his whole operation.

Francie Feeley's fish factory was a large redbrick building with tiny windows and thick-looking doors. The tall wrought-iron gates surrounding the property were decorated with elaborate fish designs, with spiky points at the top. It was very imposing indeed. As we stood outside we peeked between the bars, trying to see who was working inside.

'No one goes in, no one comes out. It's very mysterious, isn't it, buddy?' I said.

'It is, Sean. It's exactly like Willy Wonka's chocolate factory.'

'Yes!' I agreed. 'Although, Francie goes in and out a lot, doesn't he?'

'Indeed he does, Sean, many times a day.'

'So . . . he's kinda the exact opposite of Willy Wonka really.'

'That's true. It's like Willy Wonka's chocolate factory if Willy Wonka went in and out a lot and ran a small but very successful chocolate shop in the middle of the town,' I suggested.

'It's exactly like that!' Martin agreed.

We walked around the walls, desperate for an opening. We were on a clue-search. Half an hour later, we were searched out and utterly clueless. We needed to get inside.

Ping! I looked to Martin and noticed that a light bulb had gone on above his head. This always happened when Martin got an idea. It was an after-effect of the time he stuck a fork into a plug socket thinking some jelly had fallen in there.

'I see your thinking bulb's on, buddy,' I said hopefully.

'Yes, I really must see a doctor about that,' he replied, looking up.

'You have a plan?'

'I do indeed, my bearded assistant.'

51

'Assistant?'

'Do you remember that episode of *The A-Team**** when Hannibal****** went undercover as a biker to infiltrate that evil motorcycle gang?'

'Remember it? It was the finest forty-six minutes of my life!' I said.

'Me too. And it's just given me another one of my brilliant ideas that I got from television.'

'We're going to start an evil motorcycle gang?' I asked.

'No, Sean!'

'We're going do a short course on motorcycle management and take it from there?'

'Nope.'

'We're going to get tattoos of motorbikes and

*THE A-TEAM — an action-filled TV show about a group of renegades who solve crimes, kick ass and ask questions later. Not to be confused with The B-Team, who always asked questions first.

**HANNIBAL — a character from *The A-Team* who was famous for his undercover skills and beating people up. Not to be confused with Hannibal Lecter, who was famous for *eating* people up.

maybe wear some leather shorts?'

'No, but we should definitely think about
doing those things too.'

'What's your plan, Martin?'

'Sean, we're going to go undercover! We're
going to infiltrate the factory, like a couple
of fish-moles, and we're going to find out the
truth behind this big weird mysterious place!'

'Yes! I've always wanted to be in a motorcycle
gang!'

'What? Were you even
listening to me?'

'I'm going to be Dirtbag. And you can be Mild Thing. Or Hogwart. Or Roadkill. Take your pick.'

'No, Sean! I'm going to be a fish detective!'

'That makes more sense.' I nodded.

CHAPTER SIX
MEAT SURPRISE

'A fish . . . *detective*?' asked a puzzled Bridget Cross.

Martin nodded enthusiastically. 'I also like to think of myself as a Fish-Mole. Or a Private Infishtigator.'

'So you'd be my . . . spy? My eyes and ears?'

'Exactamundo, Mrs C!' Martin beamed.

'And maybe her mouth and nose too,' I added, 'if we find any edible or smellable clues.'

'So what do you think?' Martin asked her.

Bridget stroked her mousy moustache as she mulled it over. Then finally her thin lips curled into a devious grin. 'It's brilliant, Martin. Simply brilliant.'

Martin looked confused – he wasn't used to having his ideas praised. 'It is?'

'It's so simple!' she cried, 'So simple it's almost stupid.'

Martin nodded, unsure. 'But . . . it's not. Right?'

Bridget laughed – a gravelly, squeaking cackle, like a vampire choking on a whistle.

'*Nach bhfuil sé greannmhar!*' she chuckled. 'I can't believe I was actually going to fire you today.'

'Fire me?!' cried Martin, shocked. 'Just because I dropped those pork chops on the floor and never bothered cleaning them and then sold them to that old woman and told her that all those bits of dirt were a crunchy apple glaze?'

Bridget frowned. 'What? No—'

'Just because I found a rat and chased him around the shop with a broomstick and accidentally herded him into the sausage machine, which wasn't on at the time, but then I accidentally switched it on?'

'Eh? No—'

'Just
because I
dropped your
keys into the toilet when
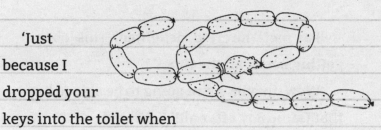
I was peeing into it, and then used that glove
you're wearing to fish out the keys, but dropped
that into the pee bowl too, so I used your other
glove to fish out the first glove and then used
your hairnet to fish out the keys?'

'No, Martin,' she said with a sigh, shaking her
head, 'I was going to fire you because I thought
you were an idiot.'

'Oh. Well, that's a relief!' said Martin.

'Phew! Thought we were in trouble there for
a sec, buddy!' I chuckled.

Bridget continued, 'But you're clearly not as
stupid as you look. Or sound. Or behave in every
way.'

'Aw, thanks, Mrs C!'

'This fish-detective idea of yours changes
everything. So I won't fire you, Martin. Perhaps
I'll even start to pay you.'

'Pay me?!' he cried, delighted. 'This job is getting better all the time!'

'Wow, maybe we're going to be able to buy that Game Boy after all!' I cheered.

But when Bridget handed Martin his 'wages', our excitement quickly faded.

'A bag of meat bits?' he said, dismayed.

'Do you know what a Lucky Bag is, Martin?' she asked.

'It's a bag of mystery sweets where you don't know what sweets are inside it until you buy it. It's basically the most exciting thing ever.'

'Well, this is a Butcher's Lucky Bag.'

We peered back into the plastic bag, looking at the collection of bones and guts.

'More like a Yucky Bag,' I grumbled.

'So . . . is this instead of money?' Martin asked.

'It's better than money!' declared Bridget. 'You can't eat money, can you?'

'No, you can't,' agreed Martin, 'And believe me I've tried!'

'You sure we can eat *this*?' I wondered doubtfully.

'What kind of meat is in here?' asked Martin.

'Who knows?' replied Bridget with a shrug, 'That's the fun of a Lucky Bag! Could be anything!'

Martin's eyes lit up, his excitement flooding back. 'Anything?! Wow! Thanks, Mrs C!'

LUCKY BAG ☘

Martin skipped home, whistling and dripping blood all the way. In the kitchen, his mother was poring over the family budget, trying to save money. So when her son presented his bloody bag to her, she beamed with delight, calculating that this would slash a whole eight pounds and sixty-three pence from their grocery bill.

'Looks like we're having Meat Surprise

tonight!' she announced happily.

The three Moone sisters looked up – Fidelma from her homework, Trisha from her latest sewing experiment and Sinead from a sugar sandwich.

'You didn't hit another fox with the car, did ya, Mam?' asked Sinead, spitting crumbs everywhere.

'No, it's not roadkill. It's from our little butcher boy!' she replied, patting Martin's head proudly.

'Hang on,' started Fidelma. 'Why's the butcher giving that meat away? Has it gone off?'

'No, no,' chuckled Martin, 'These bits were probably just too tough to go through the sausage machine.'

'What *does* go through the sausage machine?' asked Trisha suspiciously.

'Oh, you know – bones, teeth, horseshoes . . .'

Debra lifted out a misshapen bone with some fat hanging off it. 'I think this is a hip. So I guess it's hips and chips for dinner!'

The girls were not amused. 'Hips and chips?'

Martin retorted, 'Hey – at least someone in this house is bringing home the bacon*!'

Sinead snapped back, 'That is not bacon. That is bacon's ugly, freakish, inedible little brother!'

'Well, at least he's making an effort,' defended Debra, 'which is more than any of you useless lumps are doing. Why don't you get jobs too?'

Trisha rolled her eyes. 'Mam, in case you hadn't noticed, this country is in a recession. No one's hiring Punk-Fashion-Experimentalists right now.'

Debra gestured at Martin, 'Well, if this little eejit can get a job, then anyone can get a job.'

'I couldn't agree more,' said Martin. 'Shame on ye all.'

*BRINGING HOME THE BACON — a term for making money. This phrase began long ago when slices of bacon were used as bank notes and sausages were used as coins. It's also why your money box is shaped like a piggy!

'Everyone needs to pitch in,' Debra continued. 'This Christmas has got to be more of a Budget Christmas. And this is exactly what Budget Christmas is all about!' she declared, holding up Martin's guts bag.

'A bag of gristle?' sniped Sinead.

'A bag of initiative,' Debra corrected her. 'A bag of everyone helping out. A bag of the Moone family working together to make a festive, and very affordable, Christmas.'

'What's festive about Meat Surprise?' asked Fidelma.

'Well, there were cows in the manger too. And sheep,' replied Debra.

'And a donkey!' added Martin.

'I knew it – it's donkey!' snapped Trisha. 'I'm not eating donkey!'

Just then, Liam ambled into the kitchen, carrying a large cardboard box.

'How did you get on in the attic, love?' Debra asked. 'Did you find the Christmas box?'

'Yeah, slight problem though. Do you

remember that time when we saw the hole in the roof but couldn't afford to get it fixed, so decided to just pretend it wasn't there?'

Debra chuckled. '*What hole?* Hahaha!'

'Haha, yeah. Well, the thing is, a lot of stuff in the attic got wet.'

'Oh.'

Debra's smile faded as Liam set the Christmas box down on the kitchen table with a worrying squelch.

The family picked through the box to assess the damage. The Christmas lights were soaked, along with all the old decorations – not just the rubbish ones that the kids had made, but the nice ones they'd bought too. There was no tinsel. No Christmas star. Even the crib was destroyed. It was a sorry sight indeed.

I peered at the soggy Christmas lights.

'Hey, buddy, do you think if you plugged them in, that might dry them out?' I asked hopefully.

'Genius!' cried Martin, and shoved the plug into the socket.

'No, Martin!' yelled his dad.

But it was already too late – Martin was writhing around on the floor like a break-dancing bumblebee caught in a flashing spider's web.

'OHooHbbBaLLLSSS!!'

'I did not see that coming, buddy,' I told him honestly, as his sisters roared with laughter. 'But, hey – at least you've cheered everyone up!'

CHAPTER SEVEN
THE FISH-MOLE

Fresh from being electrocuted and embarrassed, Martin and I trudged unhappily along a country road. We were out for one of our famous 'grumble walks'. This was where we would go for a sorry stroll and Martin would whinge about his pathetic little life. A bargain-basement Christmas, a sugar-free lucky bag and a family that laughed at his physical torture – it all added up to a truly awful yection. During a 'grumble walk' it was very likely that stones would be kicked, heads would droop and loved ones would be cursed. If you haven't yet tried a 'grumble walk' yourself, I strongly suggest you do. It's hugely rewarding.

'Wait a flippin' minute!' I exalted. 'We need to quit this grumble and start to rumble!'

'What are you on about, Sean?'

'Remember, Martin, you're a fish detective now.'

'Oh yeah. I nearly forgot. We need to start detectiving.'

'But how do we get into that flippin' fish factory?'

'What we need is a brilliant, utterly convincing lie,' Martin declared.

'Well, that's never been a problem before,' I lied.

As we made our way to Feeley's fish factory, we put our thinking jellies to work. Soon the ideas flowed out of us like unset thinking jelly.

'How about saying that you're a fish-machinery salesman from Leitrim*?' I offered.

'What's fish machinery?'

I shrugged. 'How should I know? You're the salesman!'

*LEITRIM — this is a small, sparsely populated county in Ireland. There are no traffic lights in Leitrim. This is because they haven't yet discovered the colour amber.

'Or . . . I could pretend that I already work in the factory. And when they say they don't recognize me, I tell them that I usually have a beard but . . . it escaped . . . through a hole in my jumper.'

'Or . . . you shaved it off?'

'Or I shaved it off!' Martin repeated excitedly.

'But you don't have a shaving rash*,' I noted.

'Good point, Sean.'

'You could knock on the door and pretend to be a Jehovah's Witness*?' I smartly suggested.

'That's brilliant! Wait, I don't have any of my Bibles with me.'

'Nuts!' I exclaimed.

*SHAVING RASH — the cuts and bumps you inevitably get from dragging a rugged blade over your skin. This is why bearded people are considered to be extremely clever.

**JEHOVAH'S WITNESS — a person who goes door to door spreading the news about the life of Jesus Christ. Although, since Jesus was born over two thousand years ago, it's hardly 'news', is it?

Our brainstorming wasn't going brilliantly. We'd reached the factory gates and were standing outside, still without a plan. We dismissed 'vengeful fisherman', 'gate inspector' and 'factory collector' as being too far-fetched. We needed something less bananas.

'How about I just say that I accidentally kicked my football over the gate and I need to retrieve it?'

I looked at his scrawny little frame. 'Do you think it's believable that you could kick a football *over* a gate?'

'Fair point,' he agreed sadly.

Just then we heard a van in the distance. A pan-pipe version of a song called 'Fisherman's Blues' was blaring from it. And the stench of a tropical trout car-freshener soon hit us like a pong punch. It could only be one person.

'Francie Feeley!' I cried.

'OK, OK. I've got it! Where's my copybook?' Martin squealed as he searched his backpack. He pulled out a page and started to draw. As the van approached us, Martin drew fast and drew strong, as if his job depended on it, which it kinda did.

Francie's fish van screeched to a stop at the gate just as Martin tore the finished sketch from his copybook. 'Touchy' Feeley poured out of his fish van with a slimy slurp.

'Oh, who's this at my private factory gate? Are you the gate inspector?' Francie asked, as he strode suspiciously towards us.

'No, sir, Mr Feeley.'

'Then who da flip are ya, kiddo?'

'Don't tell him your real name, Martin! Quick, make up a fake one.'

Martin Moone is not the quickest thinker, but he tried his best to conjure a new identity on the spot.

'What? . . . My name? My name is . . . what I'm called, which is . . . my name, and that is . . . Fartin Foone.'

'Farting?' asked a confused Francie.

'No! Haha. Fartin,' Martin repeated slowly.

'Farting?'

'Fartin.'

'Right. No, hold on, are you saying your name is . . . Farting?'

'No. Fartin. As in . . . Sounds like . . . Martin.'

'This is going really well, buddy,' I snorted sarcastically.

'Oh. Well, hello, Fartin Foone!' said Francie, apparently believing Martin's lame name change. He pinched Martin's cheek with his fishy fingers and offered him his hand.

'I'm Francie, but you can call me Mr Feeley.'

As Martin shook it, Francie pulled him into a big bear hug, lifting him off the ground. Martin recoiled as the waves of fish aroma flooded his nostrils. It was as if someone had used a tin of mackerel juice as mouthwash.

'So what are you doing here, Fartin Foone? You're not another vengeful fisherman, I hope?'

Martin and I shared a look. It was a look I recognized. It was an 'I'm about to put my ridiculous plan in motion now' look.

'Nope. I'm here . . . because I won a competition.'

'Oh. Well done, you.'

'Thank you, Mr Feeley, sir.'

'What sort of competition?' He looked Martin up and down. 'I'm assuming it wasn't sports! Hahaha!'

'Haha. God, no, it was a competition to work in your factory.'

Francie stopped laughing and frowned at him. 'What's that now?'

'I won a competition to work in your factory. So here I am! Ready to go! Where do I clock in?'

'But, er . . . I wasn't running a competition.'

'Oh. Are you sure?'

'Yeah, I think that's something I'd remember all right.'

'Well, I definitely won it,' said Martin, whipping out his folded-up drawing from his pocket. 'See?'

'What's this?' Francie asked as he squinted at the sketch.

'It's a
scratch card.
You had to
scratch three
fishes to win,'
explained
Martin.

'I see.' Francie frowned. 'OK, let me get this
straight . . . You went into a shop to purchase a
scratch card. You ignored all the usual scratch
cards that have actual cash prizes, and went
instead for this one, which looks like it was
hand-drawn by a small child, where the top
prize was to work in my fish factory?'

'That's right!' Martin nodded excitedly. 'And
I won!'

'And when you went to collect this prize from
the mad newsagent's where they sell scratch
cards to children where the prizes are jobs – did
they mention anything about me paying you?'

'No, sir. I just presumed I'd be working
for free.'

Francie considered all this information. He used his fishy finger to retrace all the points of the story in his head, until finally –

'Well, congratulations, Foone!' he exclaimed as he pulled Martin into another foul-smelling bear hug.

'So . . . I can come inside?' Martin asked tentatively.

'Well, you won't be much use to me out here, will you?' Francie replied as he got into his van. He pulled a starfish-shaped remote control from the glovebox and opened the tall factory gates. Martin and I gave each other a very silent high five.

As the fish van passed us, Francie leaned out of his window.

'Just make sure you're out of here by seven bells, Fartin Foone. I don't want you getting under the feet of the night shift.'

'No problemo, Mr Feeley, sir!' Martin chirped back.

'Ha, imagine if your name *was* Farting!'

'Haha. Yes, Mr Feeley.'

'It'd be awful to be the kind of person that people always associated with horrible smells,' Francie said, shaking his head at the ridiculous thought.

The gates slowly opened and Martin held his nose as we followed the stench-mobile into stink city.

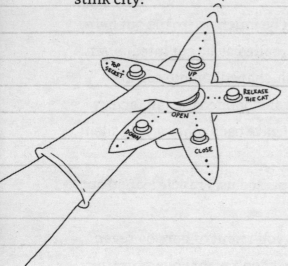

CHAPTER EIGHT
SEVEN BELLS

'Welcome to Francie Feeley's Fabulous Fish Factory!' announced Francie dramatically as he hopped out of his van. He'd parked it in a corner of the huge factory room, and Martin gazed around.

'Ooooooooh,' he said, pretending to be impressed. But in truth, the Fabulous Fish Factory was quite far from fabulous. It was disappointingly drab and run down, with rusted pipes, broken windows and peeling paint. I gagged a little as I breathed in the fish stench. The air stank like an ocean of octopuses' armpits.

'Mmeeeaaghgggrrr!' came a nearby noise. I thought it might have been my stomach preparing to puke, but it turned out to be a large Siamese cat who was peering up at Martin. She had a crooked tail and a slightly stupid-looking face.

'Hiya, cat!' waved Martin.

'Oh, I wouldn't do that if I were you,' warned Francie. 'That's our guard-cat, Fishsticks. She doesn't respond well to friendliness.'

Fishsticks hissed at Martin, baring her razor-sharp teeth. The boy gulped. Then Francie casually pulled a fresh fish from his jacket pocket and flung it into the distance. The cat licked her lips and darted after it.

'Bit of advice, Fartin,' said Francie. 'Always keep a pollock in your pocket.'

'Well, that's just common sense,' I agreed.

'Thanks for the tip, sir!' chirped Martin, and made a note of it on his hand.

Francie showed Martin around and introduced him to the other workers – two old codgers who were sweeping the factory floor. 'This is Blind-Man Bill and Deaf-Ears Dunphy.'

The two old men laughed genially. 'Haha.

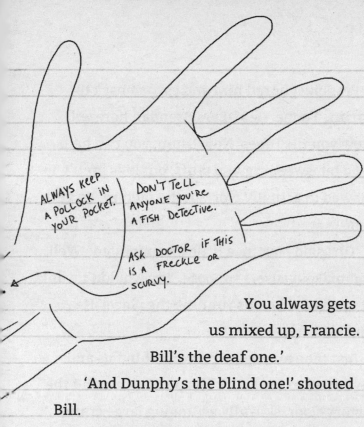

ALWAYS KEEP A POLLOCK IN YOUR POCKET.

DON'T TELL ANYONE YOU'RE A FISH DETECTIVE.

ASK DOCTOR IF THIS IS A FRECKLE OR SCURVY.

You always gets us mixed up, Francie. Bill's the deaf one.'

'And Dunphy's the blind one!' shouted Bill.

Francie looked confused. 'So it's Blind-Man . . . Dunphy? That doesn't sound right.'

'Well, you *could* just call me Brendan.'

'Just . . . Brendan?'

'Or Blind Brendan, I suppose?' he added reluctantly.

'Deaf-Ears Brendan!' proclaimed Francie. 'That's way better!'

'Except I'm not deaf.'

Francie ignored him and turned back to Martin. 'Foone. Deaf-Ears Brendan here will show you the ropes. Now listen, you can help out a bit, sweeping and stuff, but kids aren't allowed to actually work in the factory. Ya get me?'

'Oh,' said Martin, a little disappointed. 'Well, that makes sense, I suppose. You wouldn't want a bunch of silly kids running the place!' He chuckled.

Just then an engine revved behind us and we turned to see a forklift speeding around the factory floor, skilfully arranging large crates of fish packed in ice. It skidded to a stop nearby and we gasped when we recognized the driver.

'Declan Mannion!'

Martin's classmate looked over, flicking his cool, rebellious hair out of his eyes.

'Ah, you know Dec!' said Francie. 'Good stuff. Me and him go way back . . .'

He ruffled Martin's head with his stinky hands and swaggered away, giving warm hugs to Bill and Brendan as he went.

Declan climbed out of the forklift and saunterED over to Martin, lighting a thin cigar. 'I recognize you from somewhere. Do you owe me money?' he asked hopefully.

'Er, I don't think so. You took my lunch money yesterday, so I think I'm all paid up.'

'Were we in a band together? Do you play keyboards?'

'Well, if by "band", you mean "our class", and by "keyboards", you mean "nothing", then yes!'

'Our class?'

'In school. You sit three tables away from me. I let you copy my maths homework yesterday,' Martin reminded him.

'Doesn't ring a bell.'

'You stole my pencil case last week and threw it on the school roof?' said Martin.

Declan shrugged blankly.

'You fell in love with my sister for a while and were going to be my bully protector, but then I accidentally told my whole family the plan and we all got grounded, so you never managed to do it.'

Declan shook his head. 'Sorry, fella. I don't normally forget a face. But you have an extremely forgettable face.'

'That's true.' I nodded. 'You do. If it wasn't for all my reminder-tattoos, I'd never know who you were.'

GRANNY

GOES BY THE NAME OF MARTIN DOPEY-LOOKING. SMELLS LIKE STALE PIZZA

'So anyhoo,' started Martin, eager to change the subject, 'how did you get the job here?'

'Oh, me and Francie go way back,' replied

Declan as he blew a smoke ring.

'How do you know him?'

'He hit me with his van once. And we became friends after that.'

Martin gave an uncertain nod. 'Right.'

'But I knew him before that too. I fixed his plumbing for him. Didn't do a great job though, which is probably why he hit me with the van.'

'I see.'

'And I taught him how to play drums. We go way back.'

Martin nodded, wondering how old Declan really was. How many times had he repeated sixth class . . . ?

'Anyway, better get back to it, fella. Nice to meet ya!' Declan called as he sauntered away.

'*Nice to meet ya?*' repeated Martin, hurt. 'Am I really that forgettable?'

I gave him a reassuring look. 'No, of course not . . .' I glanced at my tattoos, '. . . Martin.'

Martin sighed glumly and walked off.

*

Martin pottered around the factory with a sweeping brush, trying to help Bill and Brendan. We were surprised to find the place so quiet. There was certainly no explanation for its impressive output. We snooped around a bit, keeping our eyes peeled, but there was no sign of any elves or fish-gutting robots. I kept an ear out for trained monkeys too, but the place seemed to be annoyingly ape-free.

A few minutes before seven, Francie returned. He thanked Martin for his 'work', led him outside and pressed a button to electronically open the gates.

'Bye now!' Martin called as he strolled off.

'See ya next time, Fartin!'

Francie hit a button to close the gates and walked away. But as soon as his back was turned, we whipped around.

'Now's our chance, Martin. Quick!' I whispered urgently.

'But the gates are closing!'

'You're a spy, Martin – think! What

would James Bond do?'

In a panic, Martin pulled off his shoe and threw it at the gate. This made me wonder if Martin had ever actually seen a James Bond film. But miraculously the shoe landed in the gap, jamming the gates open just enough for us to slip through.

'Yes!' I cried, punching the air. 'That should *shoe* it.'

Martin looked at me. 'What a weird thing to say.'

'That's what spies do,' I explained, 'Make quips and puns* and stuff.'

'I thought we were fish detectives.'

'Well, yeah, but I'm sure they make puns too – it's all the same general area.'

Suddenly the factory bell gave a loud *BONG*!

'The seven bells!'

*PUN – a humorous play on words. But trying to explain a pun is like trying to eat a clock. It's very time-consuming.

We hurried back to the main building and peered through a grimy window.

Once the seventh bell had struck, we heard a noise from a big fish truck that had been parked there all along. The back doors burst open and suddenly two dozen spritely, boisterous young men poured cheerily out, yawning and stretching, as if they'd just woken up from a nap. They were olive-skinned and handsome, with black hair and bohemian-looking attire.

They unloaded crates of fresh fish from Francie's van and quickly got to work, cleaning and gutting them with incredible speed and skill, singing and laughing as they worked.

Martin and I were stunned. But before we could discover anything else, we heard a growl at our feet.

'*Mmeeaauurggghgh!*'

We looked down to see Fishsticks snarling up at us with her big, stupid, scary head.

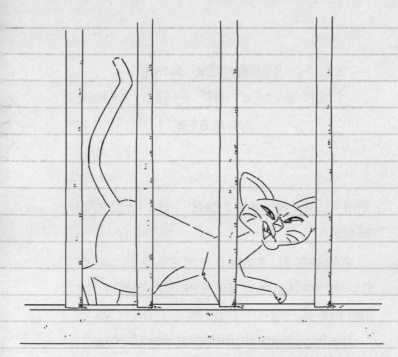

'Run, Martin!' I cried, and we bolted away.

The cat chased us to the gates, where we squeezed through the gap, grabbed Martin's shoe and fled from the factory as fast as we could.

CHAPTER NINE
FISH DETECTIVE FIELD REPORT
NUMBER 1

'You ran away from a cat?!' asked a confused Padraic.

'Not ran, P! I'd say it was more like a very speedy walk. In my defence, I'm pretty sure it had rabies,' Martin replied defensively.

The boys were huddled under the big cherry-blossom tree by the school sports field – although it had neither cherries nor blossoms at the moment, which was lucky, since Martin was allergic to both.

'You can't be too safe with rabies,' Padraic conceded. 'My cousin Fintan lost a toe when that family of squirrels he kept under his bed got restless.'

'What?' asked a stunned Martin.

'Don't worry about Fintan's feet right now –

tell me more about the fish factory.'

'Shouldn't I wait until I go into your auntie's shop later?'

'No, no, it's far too dangerous for you to be seen at the butcher shop any more, Martin. There's a lot of heat on you, and we don't want your cover to get blown.'

'I'm sure we're safe here at school, P.'

'Safe my hole,' Padraic scoffed. 'The walls have ears, Martin . . .'

Martin thought Padraic was being overly mysterious, until he pointed to a nearby wall where the Bonner brothers were putting the final touches to their latest 'work' of graffiti.

BIG EARS
JACKSON

'But if I'm not allowed to go into the shop, how will I pass on further findings from my fish-detectivery?' Martin asked.

'Well, Auntie Bridget has officially made *me* your "contact", Martin. Your "minder", if you will. The "behind people's backs go-between". All information goes through me now. I'm like "M" in James Bond.'

'Cool!' beamed Martin. 'We'll be undercover brothers from another auntie! Martin and Padraic, mission improbable!'

'That's another thing . . . I don't think we should use our real names any more. It makes things tricky.'

'Yeah, Padraic *is* kinda hard to pronounce,' Martin agreed.

'No, I mean in terms of secrecy. We should start using code names or something.'

'That's a great idea. Hmm . . . Code names . . . What if I'm . . . Fartin . . . No, wait, I'm already using that.'

'Let's just stick with the James Bond theme,

shall we? From now on,' Padraic whispered, 'you should call me "P".'

'P?'

'Kinda like "M". Except with a P.'

'But I already call you P,' Martin whispered back.

'Perfect! It'll be easy to remember.'

'Okey-dokey, Mr P.'

'And you should have a number, like Bond. But double-O seven is already taken. And double-O eight seems too obvious.' Padraic scratched his head.

'What if I'm called . . . M double-O N E?'

Padraic considered this.

'Perfection,' he declared, to Martin's delight.

'Agent M double-O N E, shaken not stirred,' whispered Martin excitedly. 'Licensed to kill. God, I can't wait to kill something. What should I kill first, I wonder? Maybe that flippin' cat. Hey, should I get a big gun?!'

'Easy there, soldier,' Padraic whispered, laying a calming hand on Martin's shoulder.

'Why don't you just fill me in on what you saw at the factory last night?'

'Sure.' Martin nodded. 'We can work out the gun situation later.'

'What else can you remember about the handsome lads who got out of the fish truck?'

'Well . . . they weren't robots.'

'Yes, you mentioned that. Anything more . . . specific?'

'Let me think. One thing I did notice was that they were pretty tanned. Come to think of it, there wasn't a single freckle among the lot of them. Just standing near them, I felt like a snowman!'

'Interesting,' Padraic nodded, scribbling in his notebook.

'I don't think they were from Boyle. They had funny accents, but I couldn't tell where they were from because I've never been anywhere BUT Boyle. The only time I've been outside Boyle was when we went on that school pilgrimage to

Knock*. But everyone there had accents because they were speaking Latin**.'

'OK,' Padraic mused. 'This is pretty useful stuff, M double-O N E.' He smiled as he continued to scribble in his pad. 'I wonder who the heck these fellas are.'

'Well, let's look at the evidence,' Martin said as he opened his evidence copybook. 'The funny accents, the bronzed skin, the music . . . I think it's safe to conclude that the fish-factory workers are a collection of boy bands from some place outside Boyle that has a tanning shop.'

Padraic looked unsure about this analysis.

*KNOCK — a small, holy town in rural Ireland where people claim to have seen the Virgin Mary appear. She then disappeared. Then appeared again, pulled a dove out of a hat, sawed a woman in half and yanked the nine of Hearts out of her sleeve.

**LATIN — an old, holy language from the Mediterranean island of Lat. The Lat people found Latin so hard to learn that they mostly communicated in whistles.

But before he could respond, the school bell clanged the boys back to reality.

'Listen,' Padraic said, getting up, 'just keep looking for clues, M double-O N E. We need more info. I gotta run now. Keep safe out there, agent.' He started to move off.

'Wait, P, where are you going? Are you in danger?'

'I need a wee before class.'

'Cool,' Martin replied, with a wink, as if 'I need a wee' was code for something, which it wasn't.

As Martin and I ambled slowly back to class, there was a feeling that this yection was showing great promise.

'Code names, killer cats, boy bands – this is exciting stuff, buddy,' I said.

'It really is, Sean. But just think what adventures we'd be having if my first-choice profession as a bin man had worked out.'

'I'm not sure that—'

But before I could finish, a leather-jacketed figure appeared from the shadows.

'Who you talking to, boy?'

'Oh, hi, Declan,' squeaked a surprised Martin. 'I was talking to . . . nobody.'

'Really?'

'Well, I was kinda talking to myself, but you always say I'm a nobody, so—'

'OK. Well, keep it that way.'

'What?'

'What happens in the factory stays in the factory, yeah?'

'Even . . . the fish? Don't they leave the factory?'

'Don't be a smart-hole, short arse. Just keep your mouth shut,' he warned, 'your head down, your arms folded, your ears closed and your hands deep in your pockets, and you'll be fine.'

'But, won't I . . . bump into things?'

'If you say another word about what goes on up there, you'll look like you bump into things all right.'

As Declan delivered this threat, the second, 'late', bell went.

'Right, kid, I gotta go.' Martin and I shared a look, surprised by Declan's class punctuality. 'I gotta see a dog about a man,' he said, correcting our thoughts.

'OK, Mr Mannion, see ya later at the factory with all those mysterious workers!' chirped Martin.

Declan turned, frustrated. 'What did I just say?'

'I'm really not sure,' Martin admitted. 'Can you remind me, please, sir?'

Declan sighed. 'I said . . . when it comes to the factory, keep your lips sealed, your eyes down, your back straight, your knees bent and your fists behind your back. *Capisce*?*'

'Cabbage!' Martin wrongly repeated, with a nod.

Declan went to correct him, but a bark in the distance reminded him that he needed to be somewhere.

CAPISCE — (pronounced 'capeesh') an Italian word used in Mafia circles to confirm that people understand what's just been said. But nobody knows what *capisce* actually means. Which is probably why there are so many 'misunderstandings' in the Mafia.

CHAPTER TEN
THE GRILLING

When school finally finished for the day, we hurried off towards the factory, eager to gather more clues and crack this case.

'I love a good mystery,' I announced happily, 'This is exactly why I always wanted to be a fish detective!'

'Me too!' agreed Martin. 'As mysteries go, I think we've stumbled on to something big here, Sean. Bigfoot* big.'

'Bigfoot? Pff!' I scoffed. 'What a phoney. I knew him when he was just Mediumfoot. Before he got those implants.'

*BIGFOOT — a legendary hairy apeman who hides in the wilds of America and only ventures out when someone calls, 'Who wants a pair of size 56 flip-flops?'

At the factory, Martin was about to ring the bell when the huge gates creaked open before us. Bill was standing there with Brendan, holding the gate clicker.

'Hi, lads!' Martin waved cheerily.

'The boss wants to see ya!' shouted Bill.

'Okey-dokey,' said Brendan, and started blindly walking off towards the office.

'Not you!' called Bill, and went hurrying after him.

Martin turned to me, looking worried. 'The boss wants to see me?'

'Wow,' I replied, impressed. 'Sounds to me like someone's getting a raise!'

'You really think so?'

'Well, it's either that or you're getting fired. It's fifty-fifty, I'd say.'

'Fifty-fifty?' Martin brightened. 'Two fifties make a hundred! So that means I've got a hundred-per-cent chance of not getting fired!'

That didn't sound quite right to me. But we'd been doing a lot of napping during maths class so I wasn't really in a position to argue. 'I'm liking our odds, Martin!'

We high-fived happily and strode away.

Martin gave a confident *rat-a-tat-tat* on the office door.

'*Entrez!*' called Francie in a French accent, for no apparent reason.

We went into the room to find him wearing a pair of paint-spattered overalls, carefully putting the finishing touches to a huge painting on the wall. It depicted Francie as a kind of octopus swimming underwater. One of his long tentacles held a spear, which he was pointing at a lion. Which was also underwater.

'Er, you wanted to see me, sir?' asked Martin.

'Indeed I did, Fartin,' said Francie, with his back to him. 'Or should I say . . .' he turned around dramatically, '*Parton!*'

We looked at him blankly.

Francie glanced down at a notebook on the desk. 'Sorry, I meant, or should I say . . . *Martin!*'

Martin and I gasped.

'He knows your real name!' I cried. 'We've been ratted out. Someone's a rat!'

'I thought *we* were the rats,' he whispered back.

'No, we're not rats – we're fish-moles! Or some kind of . . . spy gerbils.'

Francie put aside his brushes and walked towards us slowly. 'I know that you know, Martin.'

'I don't know anything!'

'You don't know anything about what?'

'About the mysterious men jumping out of the truck and doing loads of fish-gutting!'

'Aha! You do know! I knew it! I told you I knew that you knew!'

'Oh balls, he tricked us!' I cried. 'He's an evil genius!'

'But how did you know that I know?' asked Martin.

Francie put a hand on his shoulder. 'In some ways, I've always known, Martin. I have senses, you see. Long tentacles of knowledge, like an octopus's brain,' he said mysteriously, glancing at his painting. 'And also, Declan told me.'

Declan gave a wave from the corner of the room. 'Howaya.'

We both scowled at him.

'So now – what to do?' mulled Francie. He paced around, considering his options. 'I could: A. Have you gutted like a fish; B. Have your memory wiped clean; or C. Bide my time. Do nothing about it for ages. And then, when you're least expecting it, have you gutted like a fish! Unless I've totally forgotten about it by then. Those are your options, Moone – choose now!'

Martin looked alarmed and whispered to me

urgently, 'What do you think, Sean?'

'Sorry, I wasn't listening. What was "A" again?' I kept getting distracted by that weird painting.

'Time's up!' shouted Francie. 'I guess I'll just gut you like a fish.'

'No!' cried Martin. 'Look, Mr Feeley, sir, I know I haven't been totally honest with you – about my name, or the whole . . . competition-to-work-in-your-factory thing, but—'

'You lied about the competition too?' interrupted Francie. 'But what about the scratch card?'

'It was a fake. I made it myself.'

'What are you, some kind of scratch-card forger?' he demanded angrily.

Martin looked to me for advice.

'Just speak from the heart, buddy,' I told him, 'Or else punch him in the goolies* and run. Up to you.'

*GOOLIES — for a visual explanation of this word, just take away the G, L, I, E, S.

Martin turned back to Francie. 'I may have forged a scratch card. But I'm no scratch-card forger.'

'Then what are ya?'

'I'm just a man who loves fish,' stated Martin simply.

Francie's face softened a bit.

'That's it, Martin, keep going,' I urged.

'Ever since I was a little boy,' continued Martin, 'I had a dream. A simple dream. To work in a fish factory. To smell the stinky air. To shovel the fish ice. To walk on a slippery or sometimes crunchy floor. And to follow the great Fish King. To learn his ways. To swim in his footsteps. You see, Mr Feeley, I'm just a young you.'

Francie was clearly moved by this. 'Me too, Martin,' he said. 'But how do I know this isn't more of your scratch-card fakery?'

'Don't worry, boss,' Declan assured him coolly, 'Moone won't be any trouble. He's too stupid to be a threat.'

Martin half nodded, unsure if this was an insult or not.

'You're sure?' Francie asked Declan.

'Well, put it this way – I once saw him eat a whole plastic display of fruit and not know the difference.'

Martin chuckled with amusement. 'Haha, no, that's not true. But I did once eat a whole display of fruit in a shop once. That part is true.'

'And how did it taste?' asked Francie.

'Not great. Completely juiceless. I think it had been sitting on the counter for a few days.'

Francie shared a look with Declan, then turned back to Martin and smiled. 'All right, Moone. "C" it is. I won't gut you just yet.'

'Aw, thanks, Mr Feeley!' beamed Martin with relief.

'Now let's find a proper use for you,' said Francie, and handed him a sweeping brush.

Martin was delighted with himself – until he

noticed that the brush's bristles were covered with blood.

We shared a worried look.

Gulp.

CHAPTER ELEVEN
A BOY CALLED FISH-GUTS

'Hmmm, good question.' Francie mused, 'I suppose the trickiest thing about clearing up fish-guts is brush-bristle blockage.'

'Did you even ask a question, Martin?' I whispered to the boy. A confused shrug in my direction suggested that Francie was actually answering his own question, a question he hadn't spoken out loud. Bill, Brendan, Martin and I stood watching him hold court in the middle of the foul-smelling fish-factory floor.

'Over the years, I've developed a method to overcome this nuisance. I call it the ol' sweep-sweep-bang-bang.'

Martin stared back at his new boss, none the wiser.

'"How does the ol' sweep-sweep-bang-bang method work?" I hear you ask,' Francie continued.

'Don't think you actually heard us ask that,' I murmured to myself.

'It's fairly self-explanatory,' said Francie, taking Martin's brush to demonstrate. 'You sweep, you sweep –' he swept – 'and you bang, you bang,' he instructed, as he tapped the brush on the floor, ridding it of fish morsels. 'Got it, little fella?'

'Got it, Mr Feeley, sir. But where should I sweep the fish-guts to?' asked Martin, looking around. 'Is there a big waste hole somewhere?'

'Another brilliant question, Moone! No. There is no *waste* hole somewhere. Nor is there a waste chute, nor a waste tank.'

'But where do all the useless bits of fish go, Mr Feeley, sir?'

'Moone, I don't believe in the word *waste*.'

'A junk trunk then. Maybe a scum drum? A slop drop.'

Francie shook his head as he put his hand on Martin's shoulder. 'There's only two things you need to know about me, little Moone. If you remember these things, everything I do will seem logical and understandable. If you don't, may your god help you.'

Martin listened, intrigued.

'Number one is – I love fish. I flippin' love them. If I could marry a fish and the world wouldn't judge me poorly, I would. This love means that I'm not fond of killing them. But they're so damn tasty. Look at them there,' he whispered fondly, as he pointed to a box of gross-looking trout. 'They're just crying out to be eaten, aren't they, the delicious little blighters?'

'They sure are,' lied Martin, between gritted teeth.

'If we're gonna kill them for their tasty flesh, I insist on using the whole fish. Waste is for wasters, I always say.' He gestured to a handwritten sign behind him which read 'Waste is 4 Wasters'.

'So we don't *waste* our fishy friends here, Moone. We sweep unused fish bits into this pretty little stream, where it gently flows into . . . the tasty tank of mystery.'

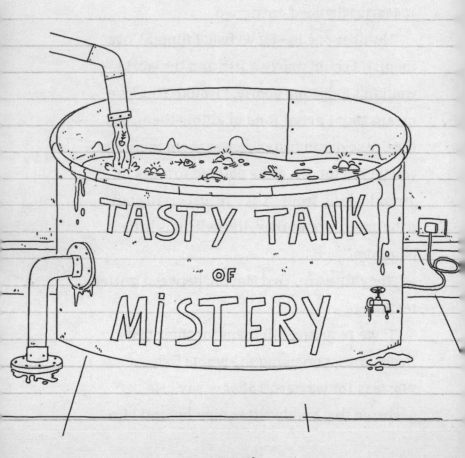

'Wow. That's . . . useful.' Martin smiled.
'Then what happens to the fish bits?'

'They have many, many applications. For example, some of the guts go through the pulping machine. From there, we add some salt, some sugar, half an onion – and that's how we make sherbet!'

Martin and I shared a look of disgust.

'That's what's in sherbet?!'

'It's fish flippin' tangtastic!' Francie exclaimed, whipping out a packet of 'Francie Feeley's Finest Sherbet'.

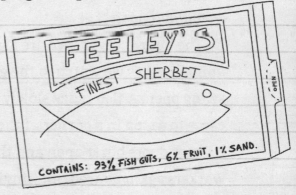

Martin and I stared at the popular packaging, aghast.

'Martin . . . you've eaten . . . *tons* of that stuff,' I pointed out to my gagging friend.

He cleared his throat and tentatively asked,

'What else is the "Tasty tank of mystery" used for, Mr Feeley, sir?'

'Loads of things! For example . . . do you enjoy marmalade?'

BBRRiiinngg. BBRRiiinngg. BBRRiiinngg.

Before a disgusted Martin could respond, the factory bell clanged loudly.

BBRRiiinngg. BBRRiiinngg. BBRRiiinngg.

'Is that the seven bells, Mr—'

Francie quickly silenced Martin with a stiff finger to his lips.

BBRRiiinnggg.

'The hour is seven. We are a go!' Feeley announced as we watched the giant gates swing open. A fish truck slowly entered and came to a stop in a corner of the factory floor. Its back doors burst open and the mysterious workers again poured out, singing, whistling and jostling with each other as they donned their hairnets and readied their fish-gutting tools.

'There they are, Martin, the men of mystery.

Time to gather some intel*, M double-O N E,' I suggested in my best secret-agent voice.

'Mr Feeley, sir? Who are those men?'

'Just the finest fish-gutters this little world has ever produced,' answered Francie.

'I don't think I've ever seen them around town. Are they from outside Boyle?' prodded Martin.

'Hahahaha. You can say that again.' Francie laughed. 'Hahahahhahahaha.'

At the start of this laugh it sounded rather evil, but by the end it also sort of sounded like he had forgotten what he was laughing at.

'Yes, they're from out of town,' Francie said, matter-of-factly.

'Ya think maybe you could . . . introduce me, Mr Feeley, sir? It'd be an honour to meet such fine fish-gutters.'

*INTEL — short for intelligence. Mostly used by those who can't spell inteligence.

'Oh. Well, I suppose that wouldn't do any harm.'

Francie banged a broom on the floor to get everyone's attention. The tanned workers turned and stared back obediently.

'Moone, these are the fish-men. The men of fish. If a salmon needs descaling – look no further. If a tuna needs retuning – come right here. No guts, no glory, but tons and tons of delicious John Dory*.

Francie continued. 'And, men, this is the new fish-guts sweeper.'

Martin waved shyly, a little disappointed by his underwhelming introduction.

They all looked to Martin, then back at Francie. They clearly didn't understand him.

'Fish-guts!' Feeley persisted, using Martin's broom to demonstrate the act. 'Fish-guts!' he

*JOHN DORY — a popular coastal marine fish. It's also where the expression 'Hunky Dory' comes from as the male fish were considered very attractive.

repeated as he swept, then pointed to Martin.

Eventually the men nodded politely, still not really getting it.

'Fish-guts!' Martin chirped, pointing at himself in the hope of clarifying matters.

The men stared back, bemused.

'All right then!' Francie proclaimed. 'Now everyone is introduced, you best all get to flippin' work!' And he stomped off towards his office.

'Wait, Mr Feeley, sir,' Martin mumbled. 'You said there were two things I needed to remember to understand the way you work.'

'Yes?'

'But . . . you only told me one.'

Francie fixed a stare on Martin. Then a slight smile slipped across his grizzly face.

'That's right,' he said plainly. Then turned again and walked away.

'Well, Martin, it seems there's more than one mystery under this roof. I guess we'll just have to keep . . . fishing for answers!' I instantly regretted this poor joke, but Martin had stopped listening anyway. He'd wandered off to check out what the fish-men were up to.

'So . . . colleagues . . . I was hoping you might show me the *ropes*. As it were,' Martin merrily suggested. 'Under your expert guidance, I'm sure I'll *catch* on quickly.'

I expected his wordplay to raise at least a polite snigger, but the men barely acknowledged him. They paused momentarily, but continued their important work without so much as a smile.

We spent the next two hours watching the mysterious fish-gutters. Francie was right; they were wonderfully skilled. Their hands were rugged but their technique was delicate. Their fish focus was unfaltering. Their control unwavering. As they chopped and pulled and pulped and sliced, they barely raised a sweat. This was probably helped by the sub-zero temperatures in the factory, but also their brilliance seemed effortless. Like they were naturals.

As the clock hit nine, and with his hands raw from fish-bit sweeping, Martin hung up his work overalls and plodded towards the exit.

'Well, goodnight, colleagues. See you all tomorrow!'

Martin waited for even a glimmer of a response. When none came, he turned, disappointed, and started to leave. His hopes of solving this mystery in one night and perhaps making some new friends at the same time were dashed.

'Bye-bye, Fish-Guts!'

Martin quickly turned to find the source of this response. But every head was still lowered, buried in their watery work.

'Not to worry, buddy. It's a start,' I said.

'Night-night, Fish-Guts!' came another lone voice as Martin walked out, smiling.

'Wait, do they think that's your name?'

CHAPTER TWELVE
A MAN'S WORLD

By the time Martin got home that night, it was
9.27 p.m. and he was zonked. He'd completed a
gruelling day in school, followed by four hours
work in the factory. Then, excited by his new
job as fish-guts sweeper, he'd skipped the whole
way home. He really regretted skipping now.
His little jelly legs were turning to slop.

'Well, at least you've earned your weariness
tonight, buddy,' I noted.

'What do you mean, Sean?'

'You're proper man-tired, Martin. This
isn't like that time your noggin got knackered
by trying to think of words that rhyme with
orange. It's not as if you're brain-tired, like
some swot. *You* are body-tired, like
an Olympian.'

'I'm like an Olympian?' the boy queried.

'Martin, you're a schoolboy holding down two jobs during a recession*. You're on course for a silver medal at life. You deserve a nice sit-down. Now go in there and bathe in the oozing respect of your family.'

'You really think they'll ooze respect on me, Sean?'

'Of course they will, buddy. You've been out there standing toe to toe with the real world, sizing each other up like a pair of insecure boxers.'

'You're right, Sean. This is a new era, the era of the employment Olympian. Me.'

'Totally,' I agreed. 'That couch is your podium, so go watch some telly like a champ.'

Martin nodded determinedly and strode into

*RECESSION — a period where normal folk have less money because rich people spent it after they broke into the nation's piggy bank to play bingo.

the sitting room, to find his three lazy sisters sprawled out on the couch like beached seals.

'Where have you been, fish-stink?' snorted Sinead, shattering our hopes.

'It's Fish-*Guts*,' Martin corrected her. 'And if you must know, I've been slaving away at the fish factory. Like a proper workman. A man of work. Not like you ladies of leisure.'

From an armchair Liam called, 'You got a job at the fish factory? I thought you were working at the butcher's.'

'Oh, I still am, Dad.'

Liam looked confused as Martin perched

on the arm of his comfy chair like a tipsy grandmother. 'Hey, I know *you* like having *one* job, Dad, but that's just not enough for me. This body lives to work. So now I've got two jobs!'

'Ol' Two-Jobs Moone, that's my boy!' marvelled Debra, stepping into the room with her hair held high in a towel.

'Why d'ya need two jobs, ya flute?' Trisha snapped.

'Because I'm twice the man of any normal man!'

'Now hold on a minute,' Liam started, before a little kick from his wife shushed him.

As Liam turned to protest, Debra leaned down and whispered, 'Don't discourage him, love – remember a few months ago when he was digging up the garden like a demented mole and having arguments with an imaginary clown? Two-Jobs Moone is a lot better than Mad-Mole-Boy Moone.'

Liam nodded sadly, remembering that when

it came to his only son, it was important to keep expectations low.

Martin stood up, his confidence growing.

'Ladies, you probably won't understand this, but I'm body-tired. I'm sure ye've spent the day fussing over knitting or baby crosswords or whatever and that's fine. But my man-form is worn out from all my hard labour and now I'd like to take my rightful place as king of the couch.'

The whole room stared back at him, unmoved.

'So . . . if ye wouldn't mind evacuating yourselves from my comfy throne, turning the telly over to *MacGyver* and allowing me some quiet time, I'd thank you kindly.'

As Martin waited for the girls to move, their facial expressions began to change from confusion to amusement. It seemed his demand wasn't even being taken seriously enough to draw anger.

Just as a collective giggle of rejection

surfaced, Liam cleared his throat and muttered, 'Seems only fair.'

'What?!! You're joking! Shaddup, Dad, just shaddup now!!' the girls squealed in unison.

'A working man does need to relax,' Debra added, to their dismay.

'Are you mad, Mam?' Fidelma yelped. '*Dynasty** is about to start.'

'Now, now, girls, ye can watch *Dynasty* another time. Your brother is no longer digging up the garden and chasing clowns, so he needs our respect before he goes mad again.'

The girls looked to their parents in turn, searching for some sense of reason on their tired old faces. But Liam and Debra were fresh out of logic that evening and motioned for the TV remote to be handed over.

'This is so unfair!' yelled Fidelma, throwing

*DYNASTY — a popular American TV show where posh women would argue over who had the fanciest shoulder pads.

121

the remote control at her brother. To his own surprise, after a little fumble, Martin actually managed to catch it.

'Sorry, ladies. It's a man's world.'

'We'll see about that,' Sinead snarled back.

As the lady seals flopped from the couch to the floor, defeated, Martin sighed deeply and switched channel in triumph.

Seeing this, Liam and Debra shared a look that suggested uncertainty about their new strategy.

As Martin happily hummed along to the *MacGyver* theme tune, his three sisters glared at him, clearly eager to take their baby brother down a peg or two.

'Wow . . . you're working so hard,' said Trisha sweetly.

'Yes, Trisha, I sure am. But a man's gotta do what a man's gotta do.'

'Must really take up a lot of time, all this manliness,' Sinead added.

'My day is indeed stretched thin, Sinead, but

where there's a willy there's a way.' He giggled.

The girls shook their heads at this. It was clear to me by this point that his sisters were up to something, but Martin was so engrossed in MacGyver's exploits that he failed to spot it. Then Fidelma delivered the knockout punch to my dozy Olympian.

'It's so amazing that you find the time to do your homework too.'

Martin swallowed hard. 'Homework?'

The mood in the room shifted. As smiles crept across the seal faces of his devious siblings, Martin felt his parents' eyes burrowing into him.

'Up!' ordered Liam.

'But, Dad, MacGyver's in danger—'

'Martin – Homework – Now!' his mother clanged.

Suddenly dethroned, Martin's shoulders sagged as he slopped off the couch and trudged off towards his room.

'Don't worry, buddy,' I said with a smile.

'Every prince has to deal with pesky peasants.'

Martin shrugged, resigned, but before he'd even reached the sitting-room door, Sinead had snatched the remote and turned the TV back to *Dynasty*.

Sensing his moment had come, Liam proffered, 'I don't suppose I could watch . . . my water-colouring programme now?'

'NO!' barked the ladies.

'Man's world, my flippin' foot,' he grumbled to himself quietly, and slunk off to eat some biscuits in his workshop.

CHAPTER THIRTEEN
PRINCESS MARTINA

If there's one thing Irish people love, it's old sayings. 'Red sky at night, we left the oven alight', 'A finger on your hand is worth two on your foot' – that sort of thing. But the one that always confused me the most was 'Hell hath no fury like a woman scorned'!

Now, I'm no 'saying scientist'. I'm barely even a mumbling expert. But does that basically mean that all the worst stuff in hell – fire-breathing sharks, lava lizards, torture trampolines – is nothing compared to a grumpy girl?

If so, then this was worrying, because Martin and I happened to share a house with three grumpy girls. And after his little 'man speech' and '*Dynasty*-interrupting' the previous night, they were feeling most definitely scorned.

The next morning, Martin's sisters decided to put an end to his newfound manliness – through the lesser-known art of a 'Revenge Makeover'.

Martin was in bed, fast asleep. And as he lay there, his stupid little face was being gently graffitied. The three girls loomed over him, quietly working away with a selection of eyeshadows, lipsticks and blushers.

'Wake up, Martin!' I hollered. 'You're being beautified!'

But all the extra work at the factory had made him even dozier than usual, and he continued to snore away. He'd snoozed through his alarm clock, as well as his mother's morning yells, and was now paying the price for his sleep-fest.

It was seven minutes to nine, and Martin's eyelids were painted an emerald green, his cheeks glowed with rouge* and his lips were a glistening pink.

*ROUGE — a kind of blusher used to redden the cheeks, often worn by old people so that no one mistakes them for a corpse.

'That's enough eyeshadow, Sinead,' whispered Fidelma.

The girls were careful not to apply too much make-up, because if they did, then everyone would know that this was their doing. And that simply wasn't evil enough for them.

'We've got to doll him up just the right amount,' whispered Trisha, 'so that it looks as if he's done it himself.'

They all cackled at this.

'Oh, you people are the worst!' I wailed.

'Enjoy school, Princess Martina,' whispered Sinead, as they gave him the finishing touches and then slipped away like serpents, slithering off to their school.

'MARTIN!!!' I roared. And finally he stirred.

'Flippin' balls!' he squealed, gaping at his alarm clock. 'It's six minutes to nine! Why didn't you wake me, Sean?'

'Into the bathroom, buddy! We've got a lot of scrubbing to do—'

'Oh, I've no time for a wash today, Sean! And no time to imagine you either. I'm late!'

'What? But—'

POP!

I vanished.

And suddenly I was no longer in the

Moone home, but instead found myself in the Imaginary Friends' break room.

Soothing music was playing quietly and a few of the IFs lay in hammocks nearby, having power naps.

'Martin! Imagine me, you fool! You're in great danger!' I called.

But nothing happened.

A friendly ogre in a tuxedo wandered over with a tray. 'Cup of rumble juice and a foot massage, Mr Murphy?'

I paused for a moment. Well, if Martin was too stupid to imagine me, then what else could I do?

'What the heck,' I said, kicking off my shoes. 'Give me the works, Keith!'

I sat back and he began to pleasantly pummel my feet.

Martin filled me in later on what happened. I'd hoped that his fancy face might go unnoticed, but sadly that wasn't the case. As he hurried into school, the weirdness began right away.

'Hey, beautiful!' came the first catcall.

'Eh. Hey . . . Alan,' replied a confused Martin.

As he jogged down the corridor, a boy began singing at him. *'Do you really want to hurt me?*'*

*'**DO YOU REALLY WANT TO HURT ME?**' — a pop song sung by Boy George, who wore lots of make-up and sometimes dressed like a girl, but called himself 'Boy' so he'd never have to queue for the ladies' toilets.

Martin gave an uncertain nod. 'Yes, a strong tune, Tommy.'

There were more weird whistles and confusing calls of 'Ooh la la' before finally Martin rounded a corner to find the friendly face of Padraic.

'Morning, Agent M double-O N E.'

'Padraic!' exclaimed Martin. 'Why is everyone acting so weird?'

Padraic rubbed his pudgy chin, pondering this deep question. 'Well, Martin, we're at the point in our lives when adolescence and manhood are fighting for supremacy in our ever-changing boy-vessels—'

'I mean, *today*!' interrupted Martin, 'Why is everyone acting so weird to me *today*?'

'Oh. Probably cos you're wearing make-up,' said Padraic with a shrug.

'WHAT?!'

Martin bolted to his locker and whipped open the door, gawking into a little mirror that he normally used for 'snot checks'.

'Argghhhhhh!' he screamed.

'All right, Madonna?' sniggered the Bonner brothers as they sauntered past.

Martin covered his face in shame.

'I kinda like it.' Padraic smiled pleasantly.

When Martin finally got a chance to wash his face, he scrubbed it so hard that he even removed four of his freckles. But that didn't stop the slagging – the catcalls kept coming all during lunch break.

'Hey, good lookin'!'

'Nice lipstick, dipstick!'

But Martin tried to ignore his idiotic classmates, focusing instead on Operation Fish Factory.

'So what new information have you got for me, M double-O N E?' asked Padraic.

'Well, Mr P, you'll be glad to hear that I survived some tough questioning yesterday, and I'm now a fully fledged fish-factory fella. I'm even on the payroll!'

'Really? They're paying you?'

'Well, not exactly. But I can have all the sherbet I can eat.'

'They told you that?'

'Well, not exactly. But I can have all the sherbet I can steal.'

Padraic looked concerned. 'Look, M double-O N E. We all like sherbet. None more than me, with its strange fishy tang. But don't forget you're on a mission here. We need intel. Facts. And, also, some of that sherbet.'

'Oh, don't worry,' Martin assured him. 'I've got my Fish Detective Field Report Number 2 right here!'

He whipped out his copybook and scanned his notes.

'Ah yes. This is great,' Martin began excitedly. 'So the break room has a vending machine. And if you whack it really hard in the top right corner—'

'It opens some kind of secret passage where the fish-gutters are hiding?' interrupted Padraic eagerly.

'Eh, no. Even better! It gives you a free bag of Skiffles!'

Padraic rolled his eyes in frustration. 'Skiffles? Sherbet? You're supposed to be finding out about the fish-gutters!' he snapped impatiently. 'Who are those guys? Where are they from? Dig deeper, Agent Moone. Follow your fish nose, keep your eye on the prize and you'll be well rewarded.' Padraic glanced around secretively, then handed Martin a bag of meat bits.

'Oh. Thanks, P.'

'Trust me, there's a lot more where that came from,' Padraic murmured with a wink.

'Where did it come from?'

'My locker.'

'I thought so. It's really starting to stink up the corridor.'

'I know. It's awful,' agreed Padraic. 'I really need some kind of a cooler box.'

CHAPTER FOURTEEN
THE WALL

'Flippin' sisters!' grumbled Martin, as he trudged down the country lane on his way home from school. 'I can't believe they sabotaged my face like that, Sean. All because of my cursed love for sleep.'

He stopped to wave his fist at the sky. 'Curse you, Sleep!'

But then he sagged again. 'Ah, who am I kiddin'? I can't be mad at Sleep. I should be mad at you, Sean! Didn't you know I'd get make-upped if I didn't get wake-upped?!'

At that point, he realized that I wasn't actually there. 'Sean?'

He looked around.

'Wait a second. Have I just been talking to *myself* this whole time?' He slapped his head and chuckled at his foolishness. 'Hahaha! I probably looked so silly there . . .

'SEAN!!' he yelled out.

Suddenly I was wrenched out of the warm Imaginary Friends' break room and – *POP!* – I was plonked on to the cold, damp road beside him.

'Oh. Hey, buddy,' I said, trying not to show my disappointment. 'How was school?'

'Worst Wednesday of my life! Hey, where are your shoes?'

I glanced down and realized that I'd left them with Keith. 'Oh. Er . . .'

His eyes narrowed suspiciously. 'Have you been getting a foot massage?' he snapped accusingly. 'Honest to flip, Sean, there I am, getting publicly mocked, while you're off getting a pedicure!'

'Well, I've got to do something when you're not imagining me! And that ogre fella has the hands of an angel.'

'Unbelievable,' muttered Martin, and walked off in a huff.

I hurried after him in my bare feet, hopping over puddles and pointy pebbles.

'Hey, buddy – any chance you could imagine me some shoes?' I asked hopefully.

'No problemo, Sean,' he called back.

POP!

'Aw balls,' I muttered, as I wobbled after him, now wearing a pair of red stilettos*.

'But, Mam, they put make-up on me!' complained Martin to his mother.

Debra was sitting on the couch watching TV with her friend, Linda, who was enjoying her usual afternoon pick-me-up – a bottle of Chardonnay and a packet of cigarettes.

'Ah, they were probably just trying to spruce you up a bit,' offered Debra.

'Spruce me up? They turned me into a

*STILETTOS — ladies' shoes with very thin high heels. These were invented for people who find walking way too easy and want it to be more like a death-defying circus act.

137

laughing stock,' protested Martin. 'Can't we just evict them, Mam? Think what we could do with that extra room. We could finally put in a sauna!'

'Look, Martin, if you just got up a bit earlier and washed your face, this never would have happened. So just get up earlier!'

'But—'

'Hush, Martin,' interrupted Linda, 'We're trying to watch the information box.'

Martin looked at the TV. It was showing a huge wall with lots of people climbing on it, trying to smash it up.

'What's this wall programme?'

'It's the news,' replied his Mam. 'It's about the Berlin Wall*.'

'Knocking down a wall – is that news?' he asked. 'Sure any eejit could do that.'

*BERLIN WALL — a big wall that was built in Berlin to keep Germans apart from each other. They say that good fences make good neighbours, so East Germany must have thought that building a giant wall with barbed wire and armed guards would make them the best neighbours ever.

'Do they not teach you about this stuff in school, Martin? This is historic. It's the end of Communism* in East Germany.'

'Mmm, look at that big hunky fella,' murmured Linda, as she watched a burly man hammer at the wall. 'He sure knows how to handle that sledgehammer**.'

Martin watched the wall-wrecking cluelessly.

'I suppose they'll be putting up a big hedge instead?' he said.

The two ladies glanced at each other, but Debra didn't have the energy to explain. 'That's right, love. They're getting rid of the ol' wall so they can make room for the Berlin Hedge.'

Martin sighed. 'It's no wonder poor Wall Street is in trouble,' he said, shaking his head, and wandered off into the garden.

*COMMUNISM — a type of society based on equality — like when your teacher forces you to share your toys with everyone, even Smashy Simon and Billy Breaks-Everything. Everyone is equal and everything is broken.

**SLEDGEHAMMER — a type of heavy hammer invented by Father Christmas to smash up old, broken sledges. Also popular with Dads, who like to swing them around the garden and pretend that they're Thor.

'OK, let's go over this again,' said Martin, as we paced around the garden, mulling over his problems. 'I'm a working man now, so I need all the sleep I can get. But I also need time in the mornings to check my face for make-up.'

'The only solution is to somehow shorten your nine-minute commute to school,' I told him.

'But how . . . ?' he wondered, as he continued to pace.

And then it struck him.

Or rather, he struck it.

Not looking where he was going, he walked right into the back wall.

'Ow!' he yowled. 'Flippin' wall!'

And then it struck me. Because I was following him. 'Ouch, me head!' I yelped. 'Wait – that's it! The wall!'

The school wall ran right behind the Moones' back garden, and I suddenly realized that instead of following the road around the long way, we should just go over the wall! All Martin had to do was hop over it every morning and he'd be there in plenty of time, free of ridicule and rouge.

The only problem was that it was actually quite a tall wall.

A terribly terrifyingly tall wall.

But when I told Martin the plan, he got so excited that he forgot about his crippling fear of heights, piled up the garden furniture and scaled the wobbly mountain of old chairs.

Soon we were sitting atop the wall – halfway there!

But when Martin saw the long drop down into the empty schoolyard below, he gulped, remembering his height-horrors.

'You think I can make this jump?' he asked nervously.

'I wouldn't have thought so,' I told him honestly.

He frowned, determined. 'I think I can. I'm a very strong jumper.'

'Oh, you're an accomplished athlete, can't argue with that. I just don't think you've got the balls for a jump like that.'

Martin looked alarmed. 'What's wrong with my balls? My balls are perfectly normal.'

'Yeah, let's not . . . go down that road. It's more of an attitude thing, buddy. You're always a bit "safety first".'

'How do you mean?'

'Well, take your choice of imaginary friend, for example. You gave me my name.'

'Sean Murphy. An excellent name,' he said proudly.

'Most common name in Ireland, but let's not get hung up on that. You also gave me my middle name.'

'Caution! Sean "Caution" Murphy. As in, careful who you're messing with, fool. Caution!'

'Yeah. Remind me – who is Padraic's imaginary friend?'

'Legendary wrestler Crunchie "Danger" Haystacks.'

'*Danger.* You hear what I'm saying? Padraic would have already made this jump, carrying Crunchie on his back like a ThunderCat*, no doubt. Whereas here you are, bickering with a man wearing ladies' shoes.'

Martin sighed glumly. He knew he'd never

THUNDERCATS — a cartoon about a group of warrior cat-people whose only weakness was being tickled under the chin.

make that jump, and so climbed back down the
wobbly tower.

He stood there, defeated. But then suddenly
he turned with frustration and karate-kicked
the wall as hard as he could.

'Flip off, wall!' he yelled.

And when he did this, to our astonishment,
he actually kicked a little hole in the wall!

Martin examined the dent, and the plaster crumbled in his hand.

I couldn't help but chuckle. 'Lovely man, your dad. Terrible builder.'

Martin picked away more cement, then managed to pull a whole brick out of the wall and found himself looking right into the schoolyard.

An excited grin crept over his face. 'Maybe it's time we did some wall-wrecking of our own, Sean.'

I smiled at him proudly. 'Ya know, it's not the size of a man's balls that's important, buddy. It's the direction they're swinging in.'

We both nodded at these wise words, although neither of us was quite sure what they meant.

But just then the factory whistle rang out in the distance.

'Ah balls, I'm late for work!' cried Martin, and we dashed away.

CHAPTER FIFTEEN
FABIO

We managed to sneak into the factory without anyone noticing our tardiness. I thought Brendan heard us clatter into a broom by the side door, but judging by his crazed feline cursing, it's safe to assume he thought we were the cat.

That evening, Martin went about his normal duties while also snooping around for any new information. He crept as he swept, keeping an ear open for any fresh intel. But when the break-time bell clanged, we realized we were two hours into our shift, and none the wiser.

During their break, the workers pulled out a football and started to kick it around. As they flicked and kicked it expertly to one another, we saw that their foot skills were almost as impressive as their hand skills.

'Whoa . . .' murmured Martin, watching their fancy footwork in awe.

'I really feel like this is a clue,' I said. But we were both stumped.

'Who's good at football?' I wondered.

'Other Alan?' suggested Martin.

'Outside of school. I mean, in the world. Who's good at football?'

Martin pondered this for several minutes.

'Jonner Bonner?' he said at last.

I shook my head wearily. 'Maybe we should just eat some Skiffles.'

'Now you're talking!'

Martin made his way to the break room, hoping to outsmart the vending machine once more, but just then a beautiful tune caught his eye. Or rather, his ear. It was coming from somewhere in the belly of the factory. The melody was at odds with the usual bashing and crashing of the machines and general silence of his colleagues. The only radio in the building was tuned to around-the-clock shipping forecasts, so we were perfectly puzzled.

'Is that . . . music?' I asked.

'I was just thinking the same thing, Sean!'

'Funny how that happens,' I quipped.

We followed the sound of the secret song along corridors, down stairwells, into musty closets until, finally, we came to the boiler room. From outside we listened to the gorgeous guitar-playing we'd heard above ground. The exotic tune was energetic but slow, cheerful but soulful. And as we stared at the closed door, we were desperate to discover the maker of this marvellous music.

'Go on, buddy, this is our chance,' I urged.

Martin tentatively pushed the door open a few inches and shuffled his foot into the gap, trying to be as quiet as he could. We peeked inside.

In the middle of the rusty room, perched on an old fish crate, was a long-haired bronzed troubadour*, eyes closed, lost in his melody. Who was this mysterious songbird? From the side they were slender-looking. And tender-looking. Could-have-been-either-gender-looking. But then he turned his head slightly and we got a better look at this curious canary. His eyes were brown like coffee and rich like banoffi**. His lovely locks flowed over his shoulders like he was standing beneath a chocolate waterfall. Making the spectacle even more delicious, the young man was strumming a guitar that was beautifully carved in the shape of a fish. It was quite the sight.

*TROUBADOUR — a European music maker in medieval times. As they lived before hairbrushes were invented, troubadours would often sing into big turkey drumsticks, pretending that they were microphones.

**BANOFFI — a popular pie made from bananas and toffee. A tasty alternative to 'potatam' a grim Irish dessert made from potatoes and jam.

Martin now recognized the handsome man from his fish-gutting exploits above ground. He didn't know his name, but he'd noticed the other workers applauding his skill and speed on the factory floor. His nimble fingers were clearly designed to delight in different disciplines.

As he finished his terrific tune, he opened his eyes and caught sight of Martin hovering in the doorway. We'd been spotted! Just as Martin moved to leave, the man called out, 'Fish-Guts! You sneaky peaky, you.'

We feared the worst until his lips slowly curled into a smile like a piece of paper set alight.

'Sorry, mister,' Martin muttered. 'I was looking for . . . the toilet. I need to . . . do toilet things. In a toilet.'

'Maybe mention you need the toilet, buddy?' I added, shaking my head.

'Fish-Guts, I am Fabio. Stop telling toilet tales and come sit with me,' he said with a smile, as he gestured towards a nearby fish crate.

Fabio was about nineteen. His chin had a dimple so deep you could rest a bike in it, and when he blinked his eyelashes fluttered in slow motion like a hummingbird's wings in a wildlife documentary. Transfixed, Martin edged on to the makeshift seat beside him.

'Fish-Guts, I have seen you work. You remind me greatly of someone from my village. My heart skips a beat when I think of them, and seeing you before me now, it sets my rhythm right.'

'That's . . . good. What are they like?'

'Oh, beautiful. With ringlets of soft cocoa hair and a smell of the freshest roses. A ponytail sweeps over the back of the dainty dress they wear like a sleepy kitten's paw.'

'That sounds like . . . a girl.'

'Oh yes, the prettiest girl in all of the village.'

'And I remind you of her?'

'Yes, yes. Her rosy cheeks and silly little face. Same same,' he insisted, pointing at Martin's own silly little face.

Martin wasn't sure whether he should be honoured or insulted, so decided to ignore this altogether and push Fabio for more detailed information.

'And where is this village, Mr Fabio, sir?'

'Far, far away, Fish-Guts.'

'Wexford?' the boy asked.

'I come from a beautiful little place called Aldeia de Lágrimas e Peixes Mortos.'

'That's . . . catchy. And why did you leave, Mr Fabio, sir?'

'I will sing my story to you, Fish-Guts. Because I like you, I trust you and I love to sing.'

In my little Aldeia, where it never snow-a,
Every single dishy was filled with little
    fishies,
The ladies sewed us strong lines, we danced
    until the sunrise,
The best place I ever know-a was my little
    Aldeia . . .

The sad song went on for quite a while. It was forty-seven verses. I don't want to bore you with the whole thing so I'll give you the highlights:

Fabio came from a small fishing village somewhere foreign. It sounded nice. Sand, dancing, food, that kind of thing. They lived off the fish they caught and sang long songs and sold fish to other villages. Everyone was pretty happy, it seemed. There were girls that looked like Martin, instruments carved to look like sea creatures and other general silliness. Then their fish got sick. Some kind of fish-blight, I think. The bay where they sourced their harvest was suddenly empty, and Fabio and his fellow villagers began to get really poor and hungry. This was very sad. Then one day, just as the villagers had decided to pack up their things and leave, a pale man showed up on a jet ski. It was Francie Feeley! He told the fishermen that their expertise was needed in Ireland. He offered to sail them all back on his yacht to the great city of Boyle, where he would secretly employ them in his fish factory. They could send money back to their families until their fish got better and they could go home. Following a big town meeting, Fabio and his friends made the difficult decision to emigrate*. So the men bid farewell to their families and their loved ones and sailed to Ireland, where Francie told them the sun always shone and the streets were paved with prawns.

'That's a hell of a song, Mr Fabio! What a voice. Do you know anything by Bon Jovi?'

'No, sorry, I only know songs about me.'

'You're amazing,' Martin gushed.

'Hold on, buddy . . . Amazing is going a little far,' I whispered, still unsure of this foreign fop. 'He's slightly interesting. But the long lank

*EMIGRATE — when a man moves from one country to another. When a lady moves, she femigrates, and if they bring their family, they themigrate.

songs, the glossy hair, c'mon . . . All a bit much, isn't it?'

I should have guessed that, as the sole voice of reason, Martin would have stopped listening to me, but I didn't. By the time I'd uttered my last word, Martin was already trying to noodle on Fabio's guitar like a nincompoop.

'Your fish guitar is amazing too.'

'Thank you, Fish-Guts. I come here to the boiler room and play sad songs whenever I miss my home.'

'Oh. I miss my home too,' Martin said sadly.

'Oh yes? Where are you from?'

'About ten minutes down the road.'

Fabio chuckled as the break bell clanged to let them know their moment together was over.

'Wait, Mr Fabio, sir. Where are you from exactly?'

'Where am I from? The greatest country in all the world!' declared Fabio joyously.

'Ireland?' asked Martin.

'No. Definitely not Ireland. Think hotter.'

'Norway?'

'I'm guessing maybe geography isn't your strong point, Fish-Guts.'

'Canada? New Zealand? Old Zealand?'

'Let me give you a hint. We are the best footballers and fish-gutters in South America. We wear yellow, we have a carnival in Rio, we have rainforests . . .'

'Scotland?'

'Brazil!' Fabio exclaimed finally. 'We are from Brazil. We are the men of Aldeia de Lágrimas e Peixes Mortos and we are from Brazil.'

'Cool,' Martin said coolly. 'Nice to meet you, Fabio. My name is Martin.'

'Hahahahha,' laughed Fabio. '*Martin!* What a silly name. Hahaha. Good one, Fish-Guts!'

CHAPTER SIXTEEN
EAST v WEST

'They're from Brazil?! That's nuts!' Padraic whispered, aghast at this new news.

'Yup, Mr P, it's Brazil nuts!' Martin winked, delighted with his pun.

Martin and Padraic were huddled at their desk in the back of Mr Jackson's classroom. He was banging on about the fate of the Berlin Wall in Germany, but the boys were otherwise occupied.

'This is huge news, Agent M double-O N E. Do you have any proof?'

'Well, he told me. And . . . there was a song.'

'A song?' asked a confused Padraic.

'Whisht, Moone!' their teacher barked, as he flung a nub of chalk in the direction of the boys. 'Padraic O'Dwyer, can you tell me who funded the construction of the Berlin Wall in 1961?'

Padraic looked to Martin, clueless. Martin shrugged back at him, hopeless.

'Wall Street?' Padraic offered.

It seemed like a decent guess to me, but the look on Mr Jackson's face suggested otherwise. He scowled at the boys before pacing left and right in his teachery way.

'The anti-fascist protection rampart was built by the German Democratic Republic to keep East and West Germany divided. It seems they didn't see eye to eye on a number of things, so they threw up the wall to keep them from quarrelling. It's a great big wall. A strong wall, a tall wall. It's managed to stay stood for nearly thirty years, but the Germans seem set on pulling it down, so I imagine its best days are behind it.'

'Why do people want to tear it down, sir?' Martin asked, pretending to be engaged.

'I don't know, Moone. It's political correctness gone mad. It's a good strong wall and I for one think it's a real shame they're tearing it down. Some people just aren't meant to live together. It's like cats and dogs.'

The classroom of clueless boys murmured in agreement.

'But . . . at our house, my dog and cat live together,' Padraic said, confused.

'And I'm sure they're always fighting, aren't they, O'Dwyer?'

The class nodded in agreement, going along with anything their teacher said, until Trevor, usually the quietest boy in class, raised his hand.

'Our cat and dog got married!' he blurted out. 'The dog wore a doll's dress, my mam dressed up like a priest, the whole ordeal. It was a lovely ceremony actually. The cat looked unsure when we stuck a ring on his paw, but they made a commitment, and by God they stuck to it. The mistake we made was sending them on honeymoon. We presumed they'd go into a field for a few hours as a romantic getaway and what have you, but . . . they disappeared for about a week. After a lot of searching, the cat came home but without the dog. My dad went out and found her dead on the road. She was a divil for chasing cars. I don't know if the cat will ever remarry – he's heartbroken. Anyway, you live and learn.'

The classroom fell silent. It was a bizarre story, but then Trevor was an odd chap.

'Well, that just proves my point,' Mr Jackson finally stated.

'Does it though?' I said.

Jonner Bonner stuck his hand up to ask a question. As a bully, he usually only raised his hand to smack someone with it, but clearly the plight of the Germans had grabbed his attention.

'If the Berlin lads want to hang out with each other, why don't they go *under* the wall?'

Though too afraid to say anything, it was clear that the class thought this suggestion ridiculous.

'Not altogether a terrible idea, Bonner,' the teacher said, to everyone's surprise. 'Building secret tunnels has worked for thousands of years. Even our own town of Boyle retains a network of underground passages which helped Catholic children go to school during the British occupation*.'

*BRITISH OCCUPATION – Ireland was invaded and occupied by the British for hundreds of years. It's believed they came to Ireland because they heard the weather was always wonderful. This turned out to be untrue, so they left. The British retain power in Northern Ireland, where the climate is very similar to Tenerife.

'Hold on a minute!' Martin started, thrusting his hand in the air. 'You're saying there are secret passageways under the town, sir?'

'First of all – yes! There's a tunnel right under this very school in fact. Not that I want you to worry that the whole school might suddenly get swallowed up into some kind of massive sinkhole with us all trapped inside it. Hahaha. But that is definitely a possibility.'

The class looked at each other, concerned.

'And second of all,' Mr Jackson continued, looking at Martin's raised hand, 'why are you wearing nail varnish, Moone?'

Every eye in the room turned to Martin's paw. His nails were indeed painted a sparkly red. As the class erupted with glee, Martin let out a small shriek and desperately tried to scrape the varnish off.

'All right, all right, all right,' Jackson said, trying to regain some calm.

Padraic leaned over to Martin. 'I see you're still going with the lady look. That's brave.'

'Bloody sisters,' grumbled Martin, scratching at his nails. 'I never have time to wash properly in the morning and those flippin' females keep plastering me with their womanly warpaint in me sleep.'

'What shade would you call that?'

'I don't know, Padraic.'

'Crimson Blush, I'd say,' mused Padraic, admiring the shiny colour.

'Boys, boys, boys, calm and *ciúnas**!' hollered the teacher.

'I need to step out for a second, boys. Please control yourselves in my short absence,' Mr Jackson muttered, as he hastily left the classroom.

Their teacher would often leave the classroom abruptly like this. The boys used to think it was because his patience was being tested and he needed a short break to stop him

---

***CIÚNAS** – the Irish word for quiet. It's usually shouted at children very loudly, which is confusing.

from battering someone. But it turned out that the real reason he went into the corridor was to do a little fart in peace.

'Listen, Agent M double-O N E,' started Padraic, watching Martin trying to remove his nail paint with the sharp end of a compass, 'while Jackson is outside doing a bum belch – Auntie Bridget is going to be delighted about your new intel but—'

'Of course she is. I know she was worried that Francie had an army of fish-gutting robots or trained dogs or monkeys or whatever. But now we know he's just using loads of lovely foreign workers from Brazil, I suppose it's case closed.'

'No, don't you see? This info has just blown the case wide open!' cried Padraic excitedly. Martin noticed that his friend was getting a kind of evil look in his eyes. 'And once we prove it, Auntie Bridget will take that case, punch holes in it and feed it to the sharks!'

Martin wasn't quite sure what Padraic

meant, but he was starting to regret telling P about his new pal.

'Well, maybe it would be better if the case was just put away safely under the stairs or something?' he suggested hopefully.

'Listen, Martin, I know this is hard for you, but you're going to need to go back to that factory and hang out with those foreign weirdos a bit more. Get us some solid proof. We need hard evidence about these guys – who they are, where they live, that sort of thing.'

'I don't know, Padraic. I'm not sure I want to do this any more. It feels kind of wrong.'

Padraic took a photo out of his bag. 'Maybe this'll change your mind, Agent M double-O N E.'

Martin peered at the picture.

'Why are you showing me a photo of your Auntie Bridget holding a Game Boy?' asked Martin, confused.

'It's *your* Game Boy, Martin.'

'My Game Boy?!' beamed Martin, delighted.

'At least, it could be – if you play your cards right . . .'

Martin's smile faded – he was looking worried now. 'And what happens if I don't play my cards right?'

'Then it's *my* Game Boy!' Padraic grinned.

'And what happens if neither of us plays our cards right?' asked Martin.

'Then . . . she said she'd throw it into the sea.'

'Throw a Game Boy in the sea?!' I shrieked. 'The woman's a monster!'

'So . . . what do you say, Agent M double-O N E?' Padraic asked, staring at Martin. 'You ready to finish your secret mission?'

It was quite the pickle. Thankfully Martin's decision was interrupted by the return of their trouser-trumpeting teacher.

'OK, lads, back to work,' Mr Jackson ordered. 'I have finished my important business in the corridor, so please turn to page 175 of your textbooks,' he continued, ignoring the fact that we all knew he'd just been playing his own arse orchestra outside.

CHAPTER SEVENTEEN
OPERATION BUDGET CHRISTMAS

After school, Martin returned home, doing his best to ignore the catcalls and insults from his idiotic schoolmates.

'Hiya, Sparkles!'

'Lookin' good, Swish Fingers!'

'All right, Pet Shop Boy*!' yelled the Bonner brothers.

'I'm a Butcher Shop Boy!' Martin corrected them defiantly. Then he turned to me. 'Although, I suppose a butcher shop is *kind of* a pet shop.'

*PET SHOP BOYS — a pop band from the 1980s who were fond of keyboards, make-up and lasers. They often performed in pet shops and were the most popular band among hamsters for eight straight years, until the Chipmunks made a comeback.

'Kind of,' I agreed. 'One where all the pets are dead.'

Martin tried not to let the taunts bother him, but by the time he got home he was more determined than ever to put a stop to his sisters' make-up assaults. Not by actually confronting his sisters obviously – he was far too cowardly for that – but instead by shortening his morning commute. So he marched over to the annoyingly tall barricade of bricks at the end of the garden and picked up his dad's sledgehammer.

'Whoa, whoa, whoa!' I cried, alarmed.

'No more whoas, Sean. It's hammer time! This wall has tormented me enough. If I don't get rid of it, I'm doomed to go through my entire life as a painted lady!' He held out his sparkly fingernails in anguish. 'Look at me, Sean. LOOK AT ME!'

'OK, calm down, Crimson Blush. Obviously I'm all for smashing up the garden wall, that goes without saying. But we've got to be clever about this, Martin. We can't just start busting it up willy-nilly. Your parents would flippin' flip out!'

He considered this and gave a reluctant nod. 'Good point. I need to use my brains here, not my brawns*.'

To be honest, I wasn't convinced that Martin possessed either, but I kept that to myself.

'So how should we do this, Sean?'

I gave a knowing smile – the smile of a man with a plan. 'We'll do it the same way you *build* a wall, Martin. But backwards!'

He nodded excitedly. 'Brilliant! Where are my plans for that time machine?'

'Er, no – I just meant we'll do it brick by brick. Slow and steady. That's the only way we'll get away with this, Martin. We'll knock out little bits of the wall every day and scatter them around town, so your clueless parents won't even notice their garden wall disappearing

*BRAWN — a word used for strength.
Brawns — a word used by a dimwit.

IDEA FOR TIME MACHINE. NOTE—WILL NEED TRACTOR. AND SOME CLOCKS.

from right under their stupid noses!'

'Genius!' he cried. 'They'll think it's just wearing away!'

'Exactamundo! Like natural erosion!'

'Like an oxbow lake!' he added.

'A what?'

'An oxbow lake. It's a kind of lake that's formed by glacial erosion.'

'How do you know that?'

'Argh, I don't know, Sean,' he moaned, 'That bloody school has my head full of useless information!'

'Well, yeah,' I said, confused, 'like an oxbow lake. So you think it'll work?'

'It can't fail! Now let's get started on that time machine!'

'Hold your horses, Crimson Blush. All you need is a chisel.'

'Even better!'

Martin chucked the sledgehammer aside and picked up a small chisel instead. He chipped out a single red brick and popped it into his school bag. We were about to head off to fling it into the river but got interrupted by a holler from the house.

'MARTIN!' screeched his mother.

We looked at each other and gulped.

'They're on to us!' I cried. 'Abort, abort!'

He was about to sprint back to the wall and replace the brick when his mother stuck her head out the back door. 'Ah, there you are,

Martin. Family meeting,' she said, and yanked him inside.

The Moones were gathered around the kitchen table.

'OK, lads, I've got some bad news,' Debra announced. 'Christmas is just around the corner and we're still broke. So it's time to move on to Plan B.'

The girls groaned and looked accusingly at their father.

'We're still broke?' snapped Sinead. 'Why haven't you earned any money?'

'It's not my fault,' said Liam defensively. 'The signwriting business is always slow at Christmas. Everyone's making their own bloody signs, scrawling on windows with snow-spray like a bunch of amateurs. Christmas is the season of shoddy signage, is what it is!'

Sinead hung her head. 'So how are we going to have Christmas if we have no money?'

'Christmas isn't about money,' Liam reminded her unconvincingly.

'He's right,' agreed Martin. 'Christmas is about food. And presents. And having a tree in your house!'

Debra shook her head, 'No, Martin, Christmas is about family.'

'Lovely, cheap family,' agreed Liam. 'And a big ol' turkey!'

'Actually we're having fish this year,' Debra told him, 'Francie Feeley is doing some great deals.'

'Lovely, cheap fish,' said Liam. '*That's* what Christmas is about.'

'I thought Christmas was about celebrating the birth of Jesus,' piped up Fidelma.

Debra nodded. 'Right, yes. Christmas is about a lot of things really.'

'Don't forget crackers!' added Martin. 'Christmas wouldn't be Christmas without Christmas crackers!'

'Or setting the pudding on fire!' yelled Sinead, who was fond of setting anything on fire.

'Or chasing away carol singers,' grinned Trisha.

'Or watching the *Dynasty Christmas Special*,' added Fidelma.

'Or having a brandy at ten in the morning,' said Liam dreamily.

Debra raised her hands to shut them all up. 'OK, yes, we all love Christmas. But it's not going to happen this year unless everyone pitches in. And if we can do that, then I'm sure this will be the best Christmas ever!'

Martin punched the air. 'Yes! The best Christmas ever!'

'But in a low-budget sort of way,' added Liam, not wanting to raise hopes.

Martin frowned. 'So then . . . it's probably not going to be the *best* Christmas ever.'

'No, that seems unlikely,' admitted Debra. 'But it can still be an OK Christmas.'

'An OK Christmas!' beamed Martin. 'That's good enough for me!'

'That's the spirit, Martin,' said Debra. 'That's

exactly the attitude we need for Operation Budget Christmas.'

The three sisters scowled at her. 'Operation what?'

'Don't give me that look. This is going to be fun, I promise!' said Debra, and pulled out an old stocking. 'See? I have a Christmas sock and everything.'

'That better not be your Christmas present, buddy,' I grumbled, shooting a glance at Martin.

'Ah, you found my old sock!' said Liam, delighted. 'It's like Christmas already.'

Debra continued, 'I made a list of everything we need. So you can each pick one out and that'll be your Christmas job.'

No one liked this idea very much, or the idea of putting their hands into Liam's old sock, but they grudgingly passed it around and picked out their tasks.

Trisha looked confused. 'So do you want us to steal these things?'

'No!' said Debra firmly. 'You can make them. Or find them.'

'Find them. Gotcha,' said Trisha with a wink.

'No stealing, Trisha.'

'No stealing, got it,' said Trisha, and winked again.

'You keep saying it like you're going to steal.'

'Don't worry, Mam – I read ya loud and clear,' Trisha assured her, and then tapped her nose.

'What does that mean?'

'What does what mean?'

'It's my turn now,' interrupted Martin, and grabbed the sock.

I crossed my fingers hopefully. 'Please just be "Christmas Cheer". We've got enough to do already. Christmas Cheer! Christmas Cheer!'

But when Martin opened the scrap of paper, he found the biggest task of all.

'Oh balls,' murmured Martin.

'Where are we supposed to find a Christmas tree?' I moaned. 'And when are we gonna have time to get one? We've already got two jobs, a wall to demolish, a bunch of Brazilians to betray, a Game Boy to earn, and at some point we really need to get revenge on your sisters too.'

'You're right, Sean,' whispered a worried Martin. 'My schedule is really filling up!'

DECEMBER

MON	TUE	WEN	THU	FRY	SAT	SUN
1	2 SPYING	3	4 RUN AWAY FROM DENTIST	5	6 GET GAMEBOY FROM MRS CROSS	7
8 AVOID SENEAD'S BIRTHDAY	9	10 EARNING BRAZILIAN'S TRUST	11	12 MORE SPYING	13	14 READ DETECTIVE NOVEL
15 GET REVENG ON SISTERS	16 PLAY GAMEBOY	17 PLAY GAMEBOY	18 LET PADRAIC WATCH ME PLAY GAMEBOY	19	20 MESSAGE THUMBS	21
22 PLAY MORE GAMEBOY	23 CLEAN EARS	24	25	26 364 SLEEPS TO CHRISTMAS	27	28
29	30					

CHAPTER EIGHTEEN
THE SPY WITH TWO FACES.
MAYBE MORE

Martin went about his shift in the factory that night with one thing on his mind – bananas. He was particularly peckish and for some reason had a hankering for a banana.

'I wonder if there's a banana machine in the break room, Sean. Or a banana tree?'

'Buddy, forget about bananas. Remember, you have to gather some proper proof for your secret mission this evening,' I reminded him, not for the first time.

'Oh yeah,' he remembered. 'That's far more important than the banana thing.'

'Yup,' I agreed. 'We really need to sneak a peek into Francie's office before that crazy butcher lady throws our Game Boy in the sea.'

'Absolutely, Sean. Bridget is completely bananas.'

When the break bell went, Martin hung up
his gut-sweeping broom and tried to sneak
away without anyone noticing him. He wasn't
brilliant at that.

'Just heading off on my boring old break
now, lads,' he lied. 'I'll be in the break room,
or the toilet, if you need me. I'll certainly be
nowhere near Mr Feeley's office, so I wouldn't
look for me there.'

Once out of sight, he lightly tiptoed down
the long corridor. There was really no reason
to tiptoe – it was a terribly noisy factory –
but Martin liked to make things exciting for
himself.

We eventually reached Francie's office. It
took quite a while. Tiptoeing is definitely one of
the slowest forms of transport.

Martin sneaked a peek through the blinds
and saw that the office was empty. He took one
last look down the corridor and quietly crept
inside the forbidden room.

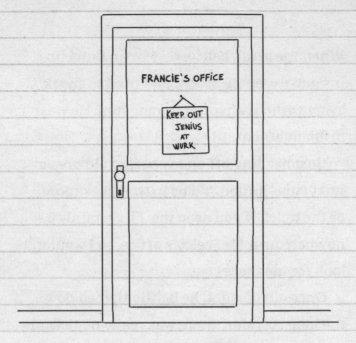

Francie's messy office was brimming with oddities. The last time Martin was here he'd been too nervous to look around. But now that he was alone, he noticed all sorts of bizarre instruments and implements that littered the windowless cavern.

There was a small piano with all the white keys missing. Hanging from the ceiling was a birdcage, but no bird. There was a jukebox which played only the greatest hits of the Bee Gees.

'It's like the garden shed of a retired cruise-
ship magician,' I noted.

'That's a very specific observation, Sean,'
Martin said.

We quickly went to work looking for intel.
We opened drawers and searched under tables
and behind filing cabinets, but couldn't find
any concrete proof. Until –

'Sean, do you see what I see?'

'Almost exclusively,' I answered.

He pointed to a large painting on the wall.
It was an elaborate image of Francie riding a
dolphin through stormy waves in the high seas.

'It's certainly eye-catching, Martin, and a little disturbing, but we're not here to critique the art.'

'No, Sean, look.' He pointed to the side of the painting's frame. There was a hinge. He pulled at the opposite side and the entire picture opened up like a door to a hidden hiding place. Sitting alone in the private press* was a solitary folder.

Martin pulled out the folder tentatively. The file inside it had a sticker on the top. It read:

THE FILE CONTAINING ALL THE INFORMATION ABOUT THE SECRET FOREIGN WORKERS IN THE FISH FACTORY

'That's handy,' I said. 'Didn't think it would be quite this easy.'

*PRESS — in Ireland, a cupboard is often called a press. Nobody knows why, and you're not supposed to ask. If you do, they stick you in a dark ~~cupboard~~ press.

'Everything's easy when you're the best fish detective in Boyle, Sean.'

'The best?' I queried. 'You're top three, buddy, I'll give you that.'

True to its title, the file contained the name, address and photograph of every Brazilian worker on the factory floor. Jackpot! Martin stuffed it into his overalls and quickly exited Francie's office before anyone spotted him. He tiptoed the whole way back. It was a long night.

As he went to grab his broom from its hanger, he was halted by a holler.

'Fish-Guts!' came the friendly call from across the factory floor.

'Oh –' the startled boy waved back – 'hi, Fabio . . . Fancy meeting you here.'

'Here . . . where we work?' asked the baffled Brazilian.

'Hahaha. Yes, no, I guess it's not that . . . fancy.'

'You funny, Fish-Guts. Listen, I see you sweep-sweep-bang-bang every night, and you good. You a swift sweeper, Fish-Guts.'

'That's . . . the nicest thing anyone's ever said to me, Fabio,' Martin babbled.

'What?!' I butted in. 'That's the nicest thing anyone has . . . ? Martin, have you gone mad?'

'But I think you ready to move up the ladder, Fish-Guts. I want to teach you. Let me uncover for you the inside secrets of the fishes' insides.'

Martin looked deeply honoured.

'I've been watching you work, Fabio. You're the best in the whole factory, hands down,' Martin said, in earshot of a few disgruntled Brazilians. 'How do you do it? How do you gut the fish so brilliantly?'

'I don't *gut* the fish, Martin,' Fabio said, flicking his hair and speaking softly. 'I just look at them with my beautiful eyes, and the fish spill themselves out in my big manly hands.'

I looked to Martin, hoping he wasn't really believing this nonsense.

'C'mon, buddy, tell me you're not buying this pile of old sh—'

'Show me, Fabio!' exclaimed the little eejit.

Despite my own misgivings about this flash fish filleter, Martin seemed quite taken with him and his glossy hair. Before I knew it, Fabio was teaching Martin the various techniques of fish-guttery. They were soon slicing salmon, cutting up cod and trimming trout like a pair of happy hairdressers. They worked in tandem for the rest of Martin's shift, until it was nearly time to go home.

'OK, Fish-Guts. Now I want you to try one all on your own self.'

'You want me to gut a fish on my own?' asked the worried boy.

'Take this bream*. Feel it. Listen to it. What is it saying?'

To my surprise, Martin held the fish to his ear.

> * **BREAM** — a type of freshwater fish. It's known to give people who eat it nightmares. Which is where it gets its name. Bad dream = bream.

'It's pretty quiet. Maybe . . . because it's dead?'

'Listen with your *hands*, Fish-Guts!' exclaimed the barmy Brazilian.

Martin felt around the scales and the tail of the deceased fish. I held my head in my hands.

'Now close your eyes, Fish-Guts. And dare to bream!'

I watched from the side, slightly embarrassed by this whole ordeal. But then something extraordinary happened. Martin, eyes closed, began cutting into the fish. He prodded and picked it, diced and sliced and removed the mess of brittle bones and gruesome guts with his fiddly fingers. I noticed that a few of the other men had gathered around to watch his artistry. Martin stopped for a moment, listening to the bream with his hands, and pulled out one last little bone, before gently laying the dish-ready fish on the counter.

Fabio smiled. 'Tonight, Fish-Guts, you are one of us,' he whispered.

Martin opened his eyes to see his crowd of colleagues as they began to applaud. I can't lie – it was a pretty special moment.

'Next week there comes a special day for us, Fish-Guts. In our village of Aldeia de Lágrimas e Peixes Mortos, every year we celebrate the day the whales came.'

'The day the whales came?' Martin echoed.

'Yes, yes. In our village we have big feast to remember when a dozen white whales came to our shore to guide us to new fishing grounds. We eat, we dance, it is like heaven, and we would be honoured if you would join us for the festivities.'

Martin was clearly touched. He'd been included as part of the family and wasn't sure how to respond. I was getting worried Fabio was about to start another long flippin' song about sad whales, so I urged him to get on with it.

'Just tell him you'll go, Martin.'

'The honour would be all mine, Fabio.'

The other men nodded with approval as the

bell went to signal the end of Martin's first night as an official fish-gutter.

'Hey, I bet we'll have . . . a whale of a time!' Martin added, completely ruining the moment.

As the men walked off towards the exit, they shook their heads at this terrible joke. But Fabio winked back warmly as he tossed his luscious mop of hair over his shoulder.

Martin waved the men goodbye, but then felt a crinkle against his chest. He suddenly remembered the secret file tucked into his overalls, and a huge wave of guilt washed over him.

CHAPTER NINETEEN
FACE BOOK

Martin was torn. He realized that if he gave
Bridget the file, it could get Fabio and the
Brazilian boys in trouble. But he really wanted
his reward. A Game Boy is a hard thing to
come by. But a good friend is an even harder
thing to find. It was quite the pickle. And not
a tasty pickle like you get from a jar. More like
a shrivelled-up pickle slice that ruins your
delicious hamburger. It seemed like the perfect
time for wise ol' Sean to deliver some of my
world-famous advice.

'Buddy, you could just remove the pickle slice
from the burger?'

'What are you on about, Sean?'

'Sorry, sorry, I think the cold weather made
my thinking jelly go solid.'

It *was* a terribly chilly morning in Boyle and we were on our way to Cross Country Meats. For some reason, Martin hadn't imagined me until breakfast time that morning, so I was eager to catch up on some good guidance-giving.

'The way I see it, buddy, you did promise to get that intel for Padraic. And it's not nice to break a promise to a friend.'

'Like that time you promised to turn me into the world's strongest man?' he scoffed.

'Actually I said I'd turn you into the world's *strangest* man. And for the record, things are progressing pretty well on that front.'

'Look, Sean, I've come up with a solution that will help Fabio and also get us that Game Boy.'

'Without my consultation?!' I asked, a little hurt.

'Well . . . I think your advice on this matter has become biased*, Sean.'

* **BIASED** — an unfairly skewed opinion formed from a personal standpoint. But an opinion is like a pair of underpants — every bum needs one.

'What?! My advice is always biased, Martin – towards you!'

'No, Sean, I think you want me to take the Game Boy because you're jealous of Fabio.'

'Hah! Jealous of him?!?! Me??! What? Who? Why would I be jealous of that eejit? His soft olive skin? His strong, skilful hands? His majestic musical mind?!' As I listed these things I was starting to agree with the little man, but I wasn't about to admit it.

'Martin, you stole that file for the right reasons. You're a secret agent, and sometimes an agent's gotta do what an agent's gotta do, for the greater good, even if they don't feel brilliant about it.'

'I agree with you, Sean, it's all about the greater good.'

He smiled as he put his hand on my shoulder. I found that a little odd, but as we approached the door of Cross Country Meats Martin pulled something from his schoolbag. It was the folder.

'You've seen sense!' I cheered.

A glint in the boy's eye gave me the impression that all was not as it seemed.

We marched into the butcher shop to find Bridget and Padraic huddled over some lanky lamb legs. Martin held the folder aloft like an Olympic torch.

'Good morning, Mrs Cross, sir. I'm happy to inform you that all went to plan.'

'*Maith thú, buachaill Moone,*' she beamed. 'I knew I could rely on you.'

She grinned as she took hold of the secret dossier.

'Yup, Mr Rely-Upon, that's me,' said Martin. 'All the information you could possibly need on the mysterious factory workers is safely in your hairy hands.'

Despite his unfortunate choice of words, Bridget looked delighted with this outcome. As Padraic threw Martin a congratulatory wink, she opened the game-changing folder. But her expression of joy quickly darkened as she perused the document.

Mick Durkin
Born in - Sligo - 1944
Skills - Fish-Gutting

Coolin O' Garvin
Born in - Wexford - 1969
Skills - Fish-Catching

Paul Mac Givney
Born in - Roscommon - 1971
Skills - Various

Lochlainn Conroy
Born in - Mayo - 1957
Skills - Gut-Catching

Martin had switched the folder! The profiles
of the workers in the factory were now all made-
up fellas from Martin's head. As Bridget turned
the pages she came to a horrible conclusion.

'But . . . all these men are Irish!' she spat.

'That's right, Mrs Cross, sir, just normal, silly Irish men with their silly Irish heads and hands.'

Bridget crossed her bony arms and glared at Martin. 'And you're telling me that these are the men who work in the factory, Martin?'

'Yup, that's them, Mrs Cross, sir. So I guess it's case closed. I have to head to school now, but I'll pick up my Game Boy later on.'

Bridget turned her wicked gaze on Padraic, who looked dumbfounded. He had brought Martin into this food fight, and he was beginning to fear he'd get caught in the Crossfire.

'Martin, you said they had foreign accents,' Padraic reminded us.

'Did I? Nope, they sound just like us. Oh, I think maybe their accents sounded funny before because . . . I had an ear infection.'

'An ear infection?' asked Bridget, disbelieving.

'That's right. I'd been swimming in the lake that week and I think I got a bad case of lake lobe.'

'Lake lobe?!' I asked, equally bewildered. He answered me for some reason.

'It's an ailment that makes your hearing go bad because of all the frog poo in Boyle Lake.'

Bridget said nothing as Martin jiggled his finger in his ear for effect.

'Anyhoo . . .' he said awkwardly, 'now that we've finally got to the bottom of this confusion, I'd best head off. Cheerio, all!'

Padraic and his auntie stood frozen, staring after their silly spy as he skipped away.

Bridget had a glint in her eye of someone who was accustomed to strangling turkeys. As her mind tracked back over Martin's story, a question trickled down her throat.

'Who goes swimming in the lake in December?' she murmured.

'Well . . .' Padraic offered, 'he has been eating a lot of fish.'

'I don't buy it, Padraic. I don't buy it one bit. Why would all these Irish men work so cheaply?' she continued. 'How did they learn to gut fish so well? And, most importantly, why do their profile photographs look like badly drawn sketches done by a child?'

She glared at her nephew. 'Padraic, Agent M double-O N E has been turned. He is no longer trustworthy.'

'But . . .' Padraic wanted to jump to his friend's defence, but as he examined the fake file, it was impossible. His auntie crashed her palm on the counter in rage. Well, it would have crashed, but there were some errant sausages lying there, so she kind of 'squished' her palm in rage.

'No one double-crosses Bridget Cross!' she snarled. 'Tail him, Padraic.'

'Tell him what?' asked her confused nephew.

'*Tail him.* Follow him! I want to know everywhere he goes, everyone he meets. Don't let him out of your sight.'

'But I can't follow him – he's my friend.'

'Ah, friendship my hoop. Friendship goes like the tides, Padraic. But *I* am family. And blood is thicker than water.'

'Right. But . . . isn't friendship thicker than blood?

'No, no. Friendship is about the thickness of cream. Or a weak gravy.'

'And family is thicker than that?'

'Oh yes. Family is like a warm bisque.'

'What's a bisque?'

'It's a kind of smooth soup.'

'So is marriage like . . . a thick soup?'

'No, no. Marriage is like syrup.'

'And an engagement . . . ?'

'Paint.'

'Hmm. What about a passing acquaintance?'

'Padraic, this is not relevant.'

'I'm just eager to learn, Auntie Bridget.'

'Fine. Milk. A passing acquaintance is the thickness of milk.'

'And . . . complete strangers?'

'Follow that turncoat*, you thick brick!!!' she hollered, as she pointed angrily at her nephew, leaving Padraic with dread in his eyes and sausage meat on his tie.

* **TURNCOAT** — a person who deserts one party or cause in order to join an opposing one. This is why most political parties no longer provide new members with coats.

CHAPTER TWENTY
THE WOOLLY WRECKING BALL

Having turned over the fake file, Martin felt
that a great weight had been lifted from his
shoulders. And this weight wasn't just the
actual file – it was weirdly heavy, so he was
glad to be rid of it – but it was also . . . guilt. All
that sneaking around and spying had made
him feel pretty bad, and given him a lot of
shoulder pain. Guilt weighs a lot – I estimate it
to be about 3.6kg – so if you're going to carry it
around, then here's a tip: don't carry it all on
your shoulders. Try to spread that guilt evenly
around your body. Get some guilt on to your
back, or your waist would be even better, maybe
by wearing some kind of Guilt-Belt.

By delivering the fake face book, Martin
had cast off his Guilt-Belt, and as his

Remorse-Trousers fell to his ankles, he now felt the cool Breeze of Tranquillity blowing between his legs.

He felt sure that Fabio and the lads would now be left alone by Bridget. And so he turned his attention to his many other tasks – starting with 'Operation Budget Christmas'.

The rest of the Moones had already made good progress. With a lot of sweat and tears and glitter, Fidelma had managed to construct an Advent calendar. However, since she hadn't found enough religious pictures to put behind all the little doors, she'd used clippings of her favourite heart-throbs instead, much to Liam's annoyance.

Sinead had the task of 'Christmas Lights' and came home one day with fistfuls of candles, which she said she'd bought from the church. This sounded a bit suspect to Debra, who grilled her about it.

'I just went to that part of the church where they have all the candles, then I stuck a coin in the slot and helped myself,' explained Sinead.

'You took the prayer candles?' gasped her mother.

'I bought them.'

'They weren't for sale, Sinead! You put in a coin to *say a prayer*. It's not a candle-vending machine!'

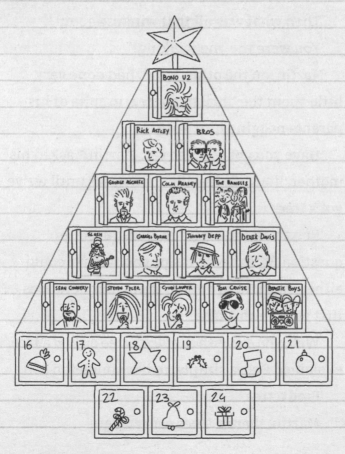

Trisha fared even worse – she stole six wreaths from doorways and two from graves. And Debra made her return them all.

Trisha seemed genuinely confused. 'I don't understand – you told me to steal them!'

'I told you *not* to steal them!'

'Then what was all that winking about?'

'*You* were the one winking!'

Martin, on the other hand, had done very little about the Christmas tree, in spite of his parents nagging him about it.

'Have you got the tree yet, Martin?' asked his mother, 'It won't feel like Christmas until we've got a tree.'

'Er . . . yes! I'm on it!' he lied. 'Just one question. With these tasks, you said we could either make them or find them. But how does that work with a tree?'

'Well, you can either *make* a tree or *find* a tree,' explained Debra simply, to her simpleton son.

'Find a tree?'

'Martin, there's trees everywhere!'

interjected Liam, 'Look out of that window. Tree, tree, tree, tree, tree,' he said, pointing. 'Just pick one and chop it down.'

'Well, not *any* tree,' said Debra. 'I don't want a flippin monkey puzzle* in the living room. It's got to be a Christmas tree.'

'But what if I can't find a Christmas tree?' asked Martin.

'Then make one!' she ordered. 'Now where's your old Lego box? I need to finish building the crib.'

Later that day we did actually try to build a Christmas tree. But the less said about that the better.

It turned out that Martin and I were way better at destruction than creation, and we had far more success with busting a hole in the back wall.

* **MONKEY PUZZLE** — an exotic, spiky tree that monkeys seem to think is a giant puzzle. They stick branches together like it's a jigsaw, but they never solve it because it's actually just a tree.

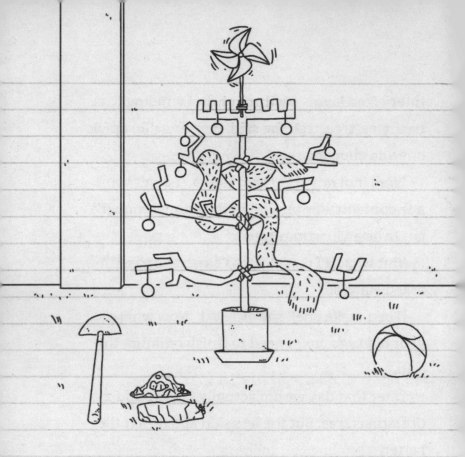

Like a gentle, woolly wrecking ball, Martin had been smashing it slowly and softly, chipping away at it piece by piece. And sure enough, his parents barely seemed to notice the widening hole. Although one morning we found Debra peering out at it from the kitchen window.

'The ol' wall isn't looking great today,' she commented to Liam.

We froze, midway through mouthfuls of Readybix.

'Was there always a hole in it?' she asked.

Liam joined her at the window. 'Ah yeah, I noticed a little hole in it yesterday.'

'Probably just natural erosion!' blurted Martin with his mouth full. They looked at him and he blundered on. 'Rain damage and the like. Rain is a terrible divil with walls. Always puts holes in them.'

Debra looked back at Martin. 'But if it was rain, why would that make a hole in the *middle* of the wall?'

Martin nodded, munching fast and thinking even faster. 'Good point, Mam. Actually, you know what? It's probably, er . . .'

'Squirrel damage?' I suggested.

'Squirrel damage!' he cried. 'That's right! I saw one nibbling on a brick just yesterday.'

'Squirrels?'

Martin nodded. 'They must be building their nests.'

'Squirrels build nests . . . ?' asked Liam.

'Out of bricks?' queried Debra.

Martin shrugged in wonder. 'That's nature for ya!' he marvelled, as he dumped his bowl in the sink.

'Mystery solved,' I said happily. And we sauntered off, leaving his parents looking bewildered.

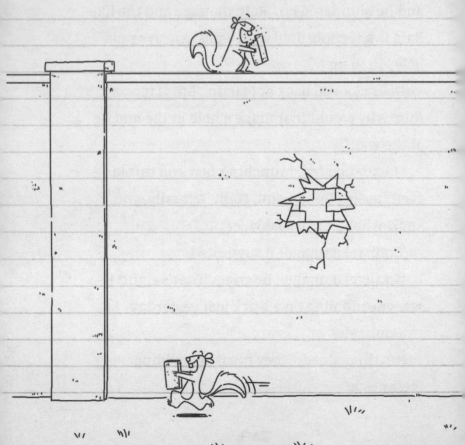

We soon discovered that there was one downside to pulling bricks out of a wall – you end up with a lot of unwanted bricks. So we had to come up with ingenious ways to get rid of them. We hid them in school lockers, tucked them in drawers, threw them in the river, shoved them in postboxes – we even went down to Wall Street and left a stack of them in Mr Ball's wall shop, Ball's to the Wall.

We developed a system for the smaller chunks of cement and little brick bits too. Martin poked holes in his pockets and filled them with fistfuls of rubble. Then he strolled around the school yard, scrunching them up and scattering them out of his trouser legs.

One lunchtime he was in the middle of doing this when he found himself standing on a metal grate that he hadn't noticed before. He kicked a little rock out from his trouser leg into the grate and heard it bounce around as it fell further and further below ground, making lots of echoey sounds. We looked at each other, puzzled, and peered down to take a look.

'Whoa . . .' murmured Martin as he gawked into the darkness. 'Have we just found the Batcave?'

'Well, it's about time!' I declared, shaking my head. 'Always the last place you look.'

'Or, wait – You don't think this is one of those tunnels that Mr Jackson was talking about, do you?'

'Hmmm. You could be right, buddy . . .' I nodded, thinking. 'Well, whatever it is, it's deep. And you know what we can do with a hole like this?'

He shrugged blankly. 'Spit into it?'

'Big time!' I agreed excitedly. 'And also – fill it with bricks!'

'Brilliant!'

But just then the school bell rang for the end of lunchtime.

Martin hopped up from the grate. 'Let's remember this for later, Sean.'

'Remember what?'

'That we found this tunnel!' he reminded me.
'I really feel like it's important that we don't
forget about this key piece of information!'

I gave a salute and he ran off.

What a weird thing to say, I thought to myself.

CHAPTER TWENTY-ONE
FESTIVAL OF THE WHALES

Martin counted down the days on the Advent calendar of handsome hunks until it was finally time for the Festival of the Whales.

It was a Sunday. But that was no day of rest for ol' Two-Jobs Moone. And as usual he was back at the factory, slogging away at the ol' sweep-sweep-bang-bang.

But Francie let them finish early that day, and the workers all piled into the back of the fish truck. With Declan Mannion at the wheel, and Martin and I beside him, we were soon speeding away into the hills of Just Outside Boyle.

The workers sang all the way – songs about whales and starving villages and, for Martin, they even sang the Brazilian version of *Jingle Bells*.

'Haha! I can't wait for Christmas, Fish-Guts!' laughed Fabio.

'Me too!' beamed Martin.

'It will be so great when we return to our village with our Christmas bonuses,' said Fabio excitedly. 'No one will go hungry and we will be heroes!'

The men all cheered. 'YAYYY!'

But Martin's face fell, and he looked back at Fabio. 'Wait – you're leaving at Christmas?'

'I thought you knew that! Once the Christmas fishes are ready, our work will be done.'

'Oh,' Martin murmured, looking crushed.

Fabio leaned forward. 'You OK, Fish-Guts?'

Martin nodded glumly. 'I just thought . . . you'd be sticking around for a bit longer.'

Fabio smiled, touched. 'Aww, Fish-Guts. We'll miss you too. With your silly little face.'

He pinched Martin's cheeks and then launched into another song, strumming his fish guitar.

His name is Fish-Guts!
So pasty white he's like a pearl,
Or like a seasick little girl.
His name is Fish-Guts!
Always talking to himself.
Like a crazy little elf.
His name is Fish-Guts!

'Well, this isn't very complimentary,' I grumbled to Martin.

But Martin was bobbing his head happily along to the music. 'Are you kidding? He actually wrote a song about me!'

I rolled my eyes as we rolled on through the hills.

Just then I spotted a familiar plump figure, wearing a trench coat and squatting in a grassy field.

'Hey, look, it's Padraic!'

Martin waved out the window and Padraic waved back, watching him through binoculars.

'That's weird,' I commented as we sped away.

'Why was he using binoculars?'

Martin shrugged. 'So he could see us better, I suppose.'

I frowned. 'You know, Padraic's been acting pretty strangely recently. I've noticed him following us around a lot – making notes, taking photos, wearing trench coats . . . You don't think he's spying on us, do you?' I asked.

But Martin wasn't even listening, he was singing along to Fabio's song –

His name is Fish-Guts!
He smells like rotten fish butts!

Finally we reached a pub in the hills where the workers were living. The whole place was decked out with Brazilian flags, Irish flags and colourful bunting. There were even fake palm trees, and big bowls of pineapples and coconuts and other exotic fruit.

'Look, Sean! Bananas!' cried Martin in wonder.

'You've got bananas at home, buddy.'

'Yeah, but these are *Brazilian* bananas, not stupid Irish bananas!'

Fabio laughed. 'Irish bananas, Fish-Guts? They'd probably look like potatoes! And taste like onions! Hahaha!'

I scowled at him. 'Well, that's just rude. I'm sure they'd be delicious! A bit oniony maybe, but delicious.'

Suddenly there was a thunderous roll of drums and Fabio held up his arms. 'It is time to give thanks to the whales! Let the festival begin!!'

And with that the place erupted with cheers and the party began.

That night, Martin had the time of his life. The workers pounded on drums and blew whistles, belting out a rhythm. They sang songs of South America and even taught Martin how to do the samba*.

'Now you teach *us* a dance, Fish-Guts! An Irish jig!' urged the men.

Martin had no clue how to do an Irish jig – but that wasn't going to stop him. So he lined them all up and led them in dance.

Now leap around and pat your nose!
Smack your belly and touch your toes!
One two three and snort like a pig!
Do the hokey-pokey and that's a jig!

SAMBA – a Brazilian dance that involves a lot of wiggling. If you don't have time to learn it properly, then pop an ice cube down the back of your shirt.

The guys all cheered, delighted that they'd learned a proper traditional Irish dance.

'We will teach these steps to everyone in our village,' Fabio told him, 'so they can all do the Fish-Guts Jig!'

As the party continued, Martin ate weird shellfish, learned new football tricks and wore a huge headdress made of brightly coloured feathers. He also met other locals that the Brazilians had befriended – their landlady, Mrs Dunphy, who stared so adoringly at Fabio that even her blind husband Brendan noticed. 'Stop looking at him! I can hear ya looking at him!'

Bill was there too, of course, trying to play the spoons along to the music, even though he couldn't hear either of them. And there were other locals who were in on the secret, like Noreen, one of the hairdressers from Scissors Palace, and Ann from Paw City the pet shop, and even Debra's best friend, Linda, who was partying it up and flirting with all the handsome foreigners.

'Wooooooh!!' she whooped, as she danced beside Fabio and slurped from a glass of Brazilian rum.

He chuckled, amused by her. 'Haha! You know, Linda, one of the Portuguese words for "beautiful" is actually "Linda".'

'Oh really?' she said, giving what she hoped was a seductive smile. 'So when you said, "Hi, Linda," earlier, you were actually saying, "Hi, Beautiful"?'

'Er, no. I was just saying, "Hi, Linda".'

Linda laughed and tossed her hair. 'Hi, Linda, yourself.'

Fabio looked a bit confused. 'Er, no, I'm Fabio. You're Linda.'

'Keep talkin', ya big smoothie,' she giggled. 'You're making me feel like the most Linda lady here.'

'But I think you *are* the *only* Linda here.' Fabio looked around. 'There's a *Laura* maybe.'

'Shut up and kiss me, ya big Linda lug,' she ordered, trying to grab him. But Fabio ducked out of her grasp.

'Time for the Whale Dance!' he called, eager to escape, and the musicians launched into a new tune.

Soon the whole crowd was dancing in a line, following one of the workers, who was wearing a big white whale head. Martin and Fabio were having a blast dancing away, but then Martin spotted me in a corner and came over.

'Hey, Sean!' he beamed, panting from all the dancing.

'Hey, Martin,' I grumbled. 'I see you're having a great time with *Fabio*.'

Martin chuckled, shaking his head. 'Is that why you're being such a wallflower*?'

I shrugged grumpily.

*WALLFLOWER — a non-dancer. The only thing that'll get them moving is to spray them with foot fertilizer and chase them on to the dance floor with snails.

'Look, Sean, Fabio is great and all . . .'

'Oh, I'm sure he's wonderful,' I said sarcastically.

'. . . but he's not my wingman,' said Martin. 'And I need my wingman. At my wing.'

I looked at him and he grinned. 'So stop moping around and let's break in those dancing shoes.'

'What dancing shoes?'

I looked down to see that I was now wearing a shiny pair of black tap-dancing shoes!

'Whoa!' I cried, delighted that he'd finally got rid of my stilettos. 'That's more like it!'

I hopped around, pulling a few moves.

Martin laughed. 'C'mon, let's have a dance-off with that whale fella!'

And we ran off into the crowd together, joining the celebrations.

As we partied, I noticed Padraic hiding behind a palm tree, spying on us again. But I was having too much fun to give it much thought. I guessed

that he must have been bitten by the detective
bug and was just copying Martin as usual. So
I soon forgot all about it, and Padraic kept
watching, taking notes, snapping photos and
eating sherbet.

CHAPTER TWENTY-TWO
THE SEVEN BELLS FALL SILENT

The next day, when Martin woke up, he was excited. And late. And looking like a lady.

Excited – because there were only four days left of school before the Christmas holidays.

Late – because he was so exhausted from doing Fish-Guts Jigs that he had forgotten to set his alarm.

And looking like a lady – because his sneaky sisters had sabotaged his face once again.

'Argh! I gotta get to school!' he yelped when he saw the time. He frantically stuck his arm into his trousers, and pulled his shirt on to his leg.

'Whoa, slow down, buddy,' I said, rubbing the sleep from my eyes. 'No need to rush. Remember?'

Martin paused, and then his eyes lit up. 'The short cut! It's ready!'

'It sure is, pal. Time to enjoy the fruits of your labour.'

'Ugh, don't mention fruit. Think I might have overdone it last night. All those pineapples have got me feeling a bit . . . explosive.'

A small fart squeaked out of him, like air leaking out of a balloon. It continued for quite a while.

I caught a faintly tropical stench and I coughed. 'Right. Well, you've got plenty of time to take care of that, buddy. And to check yourself for make-up too.'

And it was a good thing he did, because his hair was tied in pigtails, he was covered in glitter and the word 'spanner' was scrawled across his forehead in lipstick. It seemed that his sisters had abandoned the more low-key approach.

A few minutes later Sinead was pounding on the bathroom door. 'C'mon! Hurry up, Trisha! I'm gonna be late!'

But when the door flew open, she saw with surprise that it was her brother standing there – looking fresh-faced and lipstick-less.

'Gah!' she stomped in frustration.

Martin grinned at her triumphantly. 'You know what, Sinead? If you spent more time on your own make-up and less on mine, then maybe you wouldn't look like such a scabby old spinster*!'

We strutted away happily as she stormed into the bathroom.

'EUUGHHH!' she wailed, as she inhaled Martin's pineapple pong.

*SPINSTER — an old, unmarried woman who celebrates her freedom by growing out her moustache and populating her home with dozens of weak-bladdered cats.

In the back garden, the hole in the wall was looking magnificent and now cut a direct path into the school yard.

'It's so perfect,' I marvelled.

'I know,' he agreed, nodding proudly. 'This might be the greatest thing I've ever done, Sean.'

'It's your *Mona Lisa*, buddy!'

Two steps later, we were in the school yard, make-up free, with four whole minutes to spare.

And we soon discovered that we weren't the only ones who were loving the new short cut. Word had got round and loads of other kids had been using it all morning, and congratulated Martin on his handy handiwork.

'Hey, Wrecking Ball!' yelled Alan.

'Hey Alan . . . ball,' replied a confused Martin.

Tommy swaggered past, singing at him.

'*I wanna be . . . your Sledgehammer*.*'

'Oh, actually I just used a small chisel. But thanks, pal. Love that tune.'

Padraic ran over to us, excited. 'The whole school's talking about your wall exploits!' he told Martin breathlessly. 'They're starting to call you the "Dozy Bulldozer".'

'Hey, ask him why he was spying on us yesterday,' I urged. But Martin was too distracted by Padraic's face, which seemed to be decorated with eyeliner, blusher and a little lipstick.

Padraic could feel his friend peering at him. 'So . . . you're not doing the make-up thing any more?' he asked, a bit self-consciously.

'Er, no,' said Martin, confused, 'That was my sisters. They put it on me in my sleep.'

'Hah, yeah. My sisters got me pretty good too. Flippin' sisters!'

*SLEDGEHAMMER — Peter Gabriel's hit song about his favourite work-tool. It sparked a wave of other songs like *I Wanna Be Your Cement Mixer*, *Trowel of My Heart*, and *My Love Is A Wobbly Wheelbarrow*.

'You don't have any sisters, P.'

'That's cool. Whatever. I need to go and do a wee!' he cried, and ran off to the bathroom, leaving us a bit baffled.

After school, Martin headed straight to the factory, eager to see the gang again and recall the fun times from last night.

But when we got there, we found the place eerily quiet. There wasn't a single Brazilian to be seen. No sign of Francie or Fishsticks either. There was just Declan, Bill and Brendan, and a huge thawing crate of dead fish that had just been delivered.

And these were no ordinary fish, oh no. A large stamp on the side of the crate told us that these were the Christmas fish. The freshest and fattest fish of the year. Hundreds of families in Boyle had ordered fish for Christmas and they were due to be collected on Christmas Eve for all the Christmas dinners. But here they were, lying in a pile of melting ice!

'What the flip is going on?' demanded
Martin. 'These fish need to be filleted. Fast!
Where is everyone?'

Declan stubbed out a cigarette under his
boot. 'Show's over, Moone. Someone ratted out
the Brazilians.'

'What?!'

'The police raided our pub this morning,'
said Brendan. 'The lads would've been
caught – except we got an anonymous tip-off.
Someone called before the raid and told them
to scarper.'

'So where are they now?' asked Martin.

'On the run,' said Declan. 'The cops have set up a checkpoint on the factory road, searching all the cars for Brazilian fish-gutters.'

Martin was stunned. 'How could this have happened?'

Brendan began the story again. 'Well, like I said, they raided our pub this morning, and then—'

'I know how it happened!' snapped Martin.

'Then why did you—'

'Lads!' yelled Declan, shutting them up. 'The clock is ticking. The ice is dripping. All the frozen fish will thaw soon. And ya know what thawed fish smells like?'

'No, what?' asked Martin.

'Fish,' Declan explained glumly.

Just then, we heard a clatter upstairs.

'What's that?'

'Maybe it's the Brazilians!' cried Martin, and we all raced up the steps.

But it turned out to be Francie Feeley
carrying armfuls of tinned tuna into his office.
He jumped when he saw us. 'Argh! Oh, I thought
ye were the cops.'

'What are we going to do, Mr Feeley, sir?'
asked Martin.

Francie paused and looked at his faithful band
of workers. 'We'll do whatever it takes. Everyone
who has ordered a Christmas fish must get one,
no matter what. So keep them iced up, lads.
We're not going down without a fight. Right?'

'Yes, sir!' Martin saluted.

'Good stuff. Give it everything you've got! I'm
counting on ye!' called Francie, and hurried into
his office.

We followed him inside and saw that the
dolphin painting was wide open, revealing his
secret hiding place. Some of his artwork was
crammed inside it, along with Fishsticks the
cat and stacks of tuna cans. Francie squeezed
himself in with his armful of tins and started
closing the door.

'If anyone's lookin' for me, I'm in Siberia,' he told us with a wink.

'But . . . you're in your secret cupboard,' said Martin, confused.

'It's a press, Moone! And I'm not in it. I'm in Siberia!'

'But wait – What about the workers?' asked Martin. 'Fabio and the lads? You're the one who brought them here, Mr Feeley. You can't just . . . lock yourself in there?'

Francie put a hand on his shoulder. 'Worry not, Martin. Francie Feeley isn't finished yet. I've got enough tuna in here to last me years!'

And with that, he slammed the door shut.

I looked at Martin. 'Not sure that's quite what we were worried about.'

'Well,' said Brendan, trying to stay upbeat, 'at least we got rid of that flippin' cat.'

CHAPTER TWENTY-THREE
THE GREAT BARRIER GRIEF

To make sure it didn't rot, we spent the next couple of hours covering the precious festive fish-harvest in tonnes and tonnes of ice. It was unusual to see the little fella working so hard. By the time we'd finished, Martin had shovelled so much ice his nose even had a touch of frostbite. This made him look as if he'd been attacked by an Arctic vampire.

Declan informed us that the police checkpoint was on the main road between the school and the factory, so we rushed up there pronto.

We were surprised to find a small but rowdy throng of people gathered at the roadblock. There were the police, of course, securing the barricade, and Bridget Cross hovering by them, like a loyal shark. Padraic was there too, looking a little guilty for some reason, and as we approached, Crunchie Haystacks put a big paper bag over his head. It was an odd thing to do. I think he thought it hid him from sight. Even though he's already imaginary. And I should remind

you that Crunchie Haystacks is a giant of a man. The size of a haystack, in fact. So he just looked like a haystack with a paper bag at the top, like a rubbish Christmas tree. I wanted to ask him what he was doing, but we had more pressing matters to attend to.

At the barricade, as well as the group looking to catch the Brazilian boys, there was also a crowd of local protestors from Just Outside Boyle. But they weren't protesting against the Brazilians, they were protesting against the police!

Debra's friend Linda was there. As was Mrs Dunphy, who was trying to tell the police what a lovely bunch of lads they were chasing.

'They're lovely, lovely lads. Ricardo made me a wicker basket. I put eggs in it. Before I had that basket I had to carry my eggs around in my hands.'

There were many other ladies there too – weirdly they all appeared to be ladies – and they all seemed very worried about the prospect of the Brazilian guys being deported.

'Those boys really brighten up the town. With their muscles and their glossy hair and their juicy lips,' called out some quivering granny.

'Please let them stay – my husband refuses to massage my feet any more!' hollered another.

From the back, Linda piped up, much louder than the others. 'Leave them be, you dogs!' she screamed. 'If you deport those beautiful men, I swear to the Lord God I will burn your houses to the ground!'

I should point out that she was also crying. Quite violently. It was some scene. The Garda* looked ready to deploy a water cannon to cool the women down.

But there was one lady who seemed unmoved by the entire affair.

Bridget Cross was standing with one of the

*GARDA — the Irish word for Police. Because they're like guards. Sorta.

baffled guards when Martin marched over to her like a wee man possessed. She had a smug look on her face. She was even eating an ice cream, which for some reason made her even more annoying.

'Mrs Cross, sir, why are you doing this?'

'I'm not doing anything, Martin,' she smirked. 'I'm just a concerned citizen making sure our tidy little town doesn't get littered with foreign objects.'

'Foreign objects?! They're my friends.'

'Well, perhaps you need to pick your friends more wisely, little man Moone.'

When she said this, she threw a look towards Padraic, who suddenly looked pretty sheepish and bowed his head. Martin didn't spot this and kept looking for answers.

'I just don't understand what they've done wrong,' he protested.

'Well . . . they don't have the right working papers and visas and things,' explained Bridget.

'So what?'

'Well, that means they're illegal immigrants.'

'But what exactly have they done that's illegal?'

'Well . . .' she said, searching her brain, 'they're from Brazil.'

'Is it illegal to be from Brazil?' Martin asked, confused.

'No, no, it's not illegal – if you stay there.'

'So what did they do wrong?'

'They left there.'

'But they had to. All their fish died.'

'Well, I didn't kill their fish, did I?'

'No, but if your animals died, you'd have to leave, wouldn't you?'

'I run a butcher shop, Martin. I'm pretty sure my animals are already dead,' she snorted.

Martin was clearly getting nowhere with this line of questioning, but in fairness to him, when he has the bit between his teeth, he never lets go. (Unless the bit in question is a bit spicy, then he quickly lets go and has a nice glass of milk to cool his lips down.)

'Mrs Cross, sir, please just explain this to me like I'm a child.'

'You *are* a child.'

'Why are these hard-working men, who are helping their families, being treated like criminals?'

'The thing you need to understand about these Brazilians, Martin, is that they might seem pleasant and what have you, but they come over here and they take our jobs.'

'But . . . who worked in the fish factory before they got here?'

'The fish factory was closed before they got here.'

'Then . . . didn't they . . . create jobs?'

I was impressed with the little fella's logic and I could tell Bridget was getting frustrated. In fact her hands were getting so overheated that her ice cream was beginning to resemble a dairy volcano. Seeing this, the guard standing nearby tried to intervene.

'You're upsetting Mrs Cross, young lad.

Maybe you should go home.'

'Maybe *you* should go home,' Martin replied cheekily.

'Look here,' said the flustered guard, 'the law is the law is the law and—'

'And what law have they broken?'

'Well, they moved from one place to another place without the correct—'

'And in the place they were before . . . they killed someone?'

'No. They didn't do anything wrong where they were.'

'But when they got here, they stole something?'

'No, no, they didn't steal . . . They just, th-they . . .' he stuttered, 'they . . . they just weren't allowed to move here.'

'Well,' Martin said finally, 'that seems stupid.'

Bridget dropped her dripping cornet to the ground and turned to Martin.

'Maybe *you're* the stupid one, little Moone. I

know what local people want. And it's to be left to be by themselves.'

'No, that's just what *you* want. All the people I know like them,' Martin announced. 'And people love the fish too. My mam says it's way better than the rip-off ribs and pricey pork you've been peddling us for years.'

'My pork is perfectly priced!' she insisted. But Martin had already begun walking away, to the applause of the gathered gaggle of local ladies.

'I don't know why you're so upset, little Moone,' she hollered after him, 'if it wasn't for your fish-detective work, none of this would have happened.'

The ladies stopped their applause and stared at Martin.

'You made an excellent fish-mole,' Bridget continued. 'I should be rewarding you for helping me clear up the litter.'

Martin heard a gasp at this. And it wasn't just his own. He looked into the bushes by the side of the road and saw a pair of sad, handsome eyes staring back at him. It was Fabio! He'd been hiding by the Garda checkpoint and had heard the whole thing. He was devastated to learn of Martin's secret life as a spy. But not half as upset as Martin was. They shared a look of absolute despair for what seemed like minutes. Then Fabio slowly shook his head and disappeared into the trees.

Martin, the fish-gutting hero, was completely gutted. So he turned his shame on the cause of it all.

'Ya know what, Mrs Cross? You can keep your stupid Game Boy. I don't take rewards from witches.'

'Your Game Boy?' She smirked. 'I think you mean *Padraic's* Game Boy.'

Martin turned to look at his old friend. I could see the confusion on his face and the growing distress on Padraic's.

'Oh, didn't he tell you?' She smiled. 'I gave it to him for tailing you and informing me where the Brazilians were living. You two are quite the pair.'

Padraic's heart sank into his socks. As tears formed in Martin's eyes, he turned away from his old buddy and marched right up to the beastly butcher.

'Ya know what your problem is, Bridget? You're just like your manky turkeys – you're fowl.'

'You little *amadán*!' she shrieked.

TRANSLATION
'idiot!'

But Martin was past caring. He had betrayed his new pals and been stabbed in the back by his oldest buddy, and as he trudged away through Bridget's dropped ice cream he thought to himself, That's about the thickness of friendship.

CHAPTER TWENTY-FOUR
DEAD FISHES SOCIETY

It was Christmas Eve Eve.

This was usually one of Martin's favourite days of the year. It was the day the school closed for the festive holidays. It was the day when presents would start appearing under the tree and it was always a Thursday, Martin's favourite day of the week.

'I don't think Christmas Eve Eve *always* falls on a Thursday, Martin,' I pointed out.

'Really?!' The boy sighed. 'Is nothing sacred?'

Martin was sitting alone at a desk in the back of Mr Jackson's class. This was a first. For five long years, Martin and Padraic had always sat together. Like peas in a pod in a classroom. But not today. Since learning of his buddy's betrayal, Martin had spent the whole day avoiding him.

He switched desks, he hid behind the sheds at break time, he even destroyed some of his most treasured pictures of the boys together.

'We came third that day!' came a hopeful voice.

Martin turned to find Padraic leaning over from their old desk by the window. He was eyeing the portrait fondly. But Martin looked back at the sketch angrily and quickly tore it in half.

'But that was our best year!' Padraic
squealed.

'We made a promise to each other, P,' barked
Martin.

'We did?'

'Yes! We made an unspoken promise to
always stick by each other, no matter what.'

'I don't remember saying that,' Padraic said,
confused.

'It was an *unspoken* promise!' Martin
repeated.

'Oh yeah, so . . . what did we *not* say?'

'We promised to be loyal. We agreed that we
were embarking on this voyage of life as more
than friends. We were crew-mates. We knew
the stormy sea of our schooldays would batter
our friendship with waves of woe—'

'Are you making all this up on the spot?'
Padraic asked, verging on impressed.

'No! I remember this promise like we made
it yesterday. Also, I scribbled some new stuff
down at breakfast.'

'Righto.' Padraic nodded.

'We knew the stormy sea of our schooldays would batter our friendship with waves of woe and cliffs of cruelty,' Martin continued wistfully, 'but as long as we stayed afloat, I'd always be your loyal captain, and you'd always be my first mate.'

There was a long pause as Padraic took this promise on board.

'But now you're just some crusty old crustacean that's stuck to my hull,' Martin concluded bitterly.

Padraic looked pretty hurt. He'd never been called a crustacean before. A mollusc? Sure. A cockle? Every day! But a crappy crustacean? His head dropped like he'd been battered with chalk. Which coincidentally, he had!

'Whisht, O'Dwyer!' Mr Jackson hollered, raising another stick of chalk threateningly. 'I don't know what you two ladies are arguing about, but I'm trying to teach here!'

'Sorry, Mr Jackson,' Padraic muttered as he

247

turned sadly away from his old friend.

'Now, what *was* I talking about?' their teacher continued, 'Oh yes, the Berlin Wall. If I've said it once, I've said it a thousand times, boys – some people are just not meant to live together. Take these Brazilian lads hanging out in the fish factory. What do they know about Irish culture? We're best off left to ourselves. I think it'd be in everyone's interests if they swam back to their capital city of Rio de Janeiro and let Boyle be Boyle.'

'What a hunk of junk!'

The class turned to find Martin staring defiantly at their teacher.

'Excuse me, Moone?!' Jackson demanded.

'What a bucket of bullroar,' the boy mustered, taking to his feet.

'Sit down, Moone!'

But Martin had no intention of lowering himself any more. He'd let Fabio and his friends down before. He wasn't about to turn his back on them again.

'I said, sit down, Moone!'

The hushed classroom waited for Martin's next move. He had the look of someone who had planned something brilliant to say.

'I like potatoes!' he blurted.

Oh balls, I thought.

'Who doesn't? They're the best,' Mr Jackson agreed. 'What's that got to do with anything?'

'I like chips, I like wedges, I like mash, but ya know what else I like?' the boy asked the confused teacher.

'Curly fries?' Mr Jackson asked, followed by murmurs of approval in the room.

'No!' Martin yelped, determined. 'Spaghetti! And bananas. And chocolate.'

'Now you're talking my language,' Padraic said, suddenly interested.

'Sure, we could all live on spuds, and sometimes I think my mother believes we do. But we deserve more,' Martin pronounced, including the class with a sweeping gesture of his arms.

'My mind is a hungry palette and it needs feeding. Yes, sir. If we left our noggin nosh to you, you'd starve us all, you silly old head-chef!'

This brought some giggles of discomfort from the group, but Martin kept on keeping on.

'It would be like the Famine all over again. And we'd need to jump on coffin ships in the hope that our destination was more welcoming than this one.'

'Nice recall on the famine lesson, buddy,' I murmured, hoping not to put him off his stride.

'Those men are my friends. Before they were my friends, they were my co-workers and they worked hard and played harder than anyone I've ever met. And no, I haven't met a lot of people, but I'll tell you something: I can't wait to. Because people are different. That's what makes the world taste good. You have in front of you the most enthusiastic eaters in the world, and you want us to just eat spuds. Shame on you, Mr Jackson, shame on you!'

There was a collective gasp from the

classroom. Mr Jackson was fully flummoxed.
We all were. And *I'm* in his head!

'And while we're on the subject, the capital of
Brazil isn't Rio, it's Brasilia. You should be able
to remember that; it sounds like Brazil!'

Apart from a brave couple of nods, the entire
class was stunned to silence. Just as the startled
schoolman went to open his mouth in response –

BBBBBBRRRRRRIIIIIINNNNNNGGGGGG!!!!

The holiday bell rang to save Martin like a
clattering clïche*.

As the whole class jumped up in festive joy,
Mr Jackson could only watch, mouth agape, as
Martin sprang from the room. But as he reached
the doorway, a sudden call stopped him in his
tracks.

'O Captain! My Captain!'

Martin turned to find Padraic calling after

* CLICHÉ — a phrase that seems overused
or unoriginal. Unless you put the wrong
accent on the wrong letter, which makes
it hip and cool.

him. He was standing on his desk! It was quite the sight. It was like a film. Very like a film. The whole class, including Mr Jackson, was staring at this act of courage with a mix of wrath and glee.

'I'm sorry, Captain,' Padraic continued, unfazed.

Martin smiled at his first mate, knowing he couldn't stay mad at him forever. But then he noticed that Padraic was holding the torn sketch to his chest. On the back he'd written some fresh intel. The first half read 'Our new friends'. Martin looked perplexed. But then Padraic held up the other half. It read 'are hiding in the forest'.

As Mr Jackson hauled Padraic off his desk, to the hoots and hollers of the giddy grade, Martin saluted his old sea P-Dog and rushed into the corridor.

As we hastily set sail to our next port of call, Martin looked concerned.

'You think Fabio and the boys are really in the forest, Sean?'

'Actually I do, buddy.'

'But, how would Padraic know that?'

'Well, to be fair, he's pretty good at following people.' I shrugged.

CHAPTER TWENTY-FIVE
THE MERRY MEN

'FABIO!!' yelled Martin, at the top of his little lungs.

His voice echoed around the trees and we listened for a cry of 'Fish-Guts!' but no response came back.

It was the morning of Christmas Eve. And while everyone else in Boyle was battling through Bridge Street doing their last-minute Christmas shopping, Martin and I were battling through Boyle Forest, doing some last-minute Brazilian-fish-gutter-saving. At least we were trying to – if we could ever find them.

'Does my voice really sound like that?' asked Martin, listening to his echo.

'Like what – kinda squeaky?'

He nodded.

'Kinda high-pitched and squeaky?'

'Yeah.'

'Kinda silly and shrilly and high-pitched and squeaky?'

'Yes.'

'No, it doesn't sound like that at all,' I lied. 'You've got the burly baritone of a Welsh lumberjack, Martin.'

'Or like an Irish Mr T*?' he asked hopefully.

'Nail on the head, buddy.'

'Huh. I guess the echo around here must be broken.'

'Yeah, that makes more sense,' I agreed, and we ventured on.

We'd been in the forest all afternoon the previous day and had come back at first light this morning, but we still weren't having much luck. Then, as we were strolling past a huge tree, Martin yelled out again. 'FABIO!!'

* **MR T** — a muscly, milk-loving member of the A-Team. He would often say, 'I pity the fool,' which was confusing because he didn't take much pity on them at all and usually just beat them up.

'Ow my freakin' ears!' wailed a voice beside us. 'Who dis howling like flippin' werewolf?'

Suddenly the huge tree turned around, whacking me with a branch and sending me tumbling into the weeds. I looked up to see our old friend, the great imaginary tree, Bruce the Spruce.

Martin was stunned. 'Bruce!'

The tree peered down at him with no sign of recognition.

'It's me, Martin Moone!'

'And his trusty imaginary friend, Sean Murphy!' I called, hopping up from the ground.

'I know who you are, you stoopids!' barked the tree. 'You tink I some kind of brainless bush with no memory or shometin'? I told you befores – trees are de elephants of da woods, yesh? We remember everyting!'

He then turned around again, whacking me with another branch, sending me toppling back to the ground.

'Now what da flip was I jus doing?' continued

the tree. He seemed confused for a moment, but then spotted a string of ivy hanging between two other trunks like a clothes line.

'Ah yesh, my laundry! Martin, can you pass me my leafs?'

He held out a branch expectantly to the clueless boy.

'Your what?' asked Martin, who always struggled to understand Bruce's strange accent.

'My leafs.'

'Your leaves?'

'Leafs, Martin, leafs! Like briefs. But made out of leaves.'

'I think he's talking about his underpants, buddy,' I whispered, as I clambered to my feet.

'Oh right, your underpants!' said Martin, finally understanding. He picked up a giant pair of wet, leafy Y-fronts from the ground, but then looked even more confused. 'Wait – Your underpants?'

'They clean, no? You see shkid marks*?' asked a worried Bruce.

'No, no. Sorry, I just didn't know that trees wore underpants.'

'Yesh, well, some of de others prefer to wear trunks inside der trunks. But for me, it's too shweaty,' explained Bruce. 'I prefer leafs, you know? So my bottom can breathe and stay freshy-freshy. You get me?'

Martin and I both nodded politely, unsure what to say.

'Anyhoo,' I began, 'I don't suppose you've noticed thirty Brazilian fellas knocking around the place, have ya, Bruce?'

'De fishy men?'

'You've seen them?!' cried Martin.

'Oh yesh, they been entertainin' us big times.

*SKID MARKS — fart art in your under-canvas.

With der fishy songs. Us trees hardly ever gets to the seaside, so it's been real shpecial, you know?'

'Can you take us to them?'

The tree shrugged. 'Okeley-dokeley. If you guys helps me finish my laundry. I gots a lot of leafs with a lot of shkid marks to shift,' he said, and dumped a massive pile of tree knickers at our feet.

'Oh balls,' we muttered, and rolled up our sleeves.

Twenty clean cacks later, we were following Bruce through the woods. And as we strolled, a thought suddenly occurred to Martin.

'Hey, Bruce. You've actually got quite a festive figure – ever thought about working as a Christmas tree?'

Bruce snorted. 'Dis a joke? I spruce! Not fir! Bruce the Spruce! We too prickly to be Christmas trees. See?'

He poked Martin with a bristly branch.

'Ow!'

'And besides, buddy,' I added, 'Bruce is imaginary. It wouldn't be very festive if no one else could see him.'

Martin nodded. 'I suppose you're right. I guess we'll just have to chop down a nice fir on the way home.'

'What?!' snapped Bruce. 'Chop down one of my firry friends? Never!'

'But we need a tree, Bruce,' pleaded Martin. 'It won't be Christmas without a tree.'

Bruce sighed wearily. 'OK. Tell you whats, Martin. See that cone on the ground?'

Martin plucked the fir cone eagerly from the weeds.

'Plant zis in your garden. And I sees what I can do, yesh?'

'Really?'

'No promises, OK? But I'll have word with Mother Nature. She owes me a favour. Half of those undies were hers.'

'Aw, thanks, Bruce!' said Martin, and gave the old trunk a warm embrace.

'Hey, don't be such a tree-hugger,' chuckled Bruce. 'Now go say hi to your friends.'

Martin looked around and realized that we'd arrived at the Brazilians' camp! He rushed forward.

'Lads! I found ye!'

The gang of fish-gutters were living in the woods like Robin Hood and his Merry Men – but they certainly weren't looking very merry.

Martin spotted Fabio sitting in a tree, strumming his fish guitar sadly. 'Fabio?'

Fabio glanced down, but then looked away, ignoring Martin.

A short, bearded man named Paulo stepped forward. 'Fabio busy. What you want, Fish-Guts?'

Martin and I looked at each other, a little taken aback. 'I, er . . . just wanted to say . . . I'm s-sorry,' he stammered.

'You sorry? OK. All forgiven,' said Paulo.

Martin brightened. 'Really?'

Paulo laughed. 'Hahaha! No. Get lost, Fish-Guts,' he grunted, and walked off.

'I know you're all mad at me, but I want to help!' cried out Martin. 'I want to help you get the festive fish gutted! So you can earn your Christmas bonuses and save your village!'

Paulo came back. 'And how you do that?' he asked.

'I have a plan,' said Martin.

'What kind of plan?'

'A plan that cannot fail.'

'Well, let's not oversell it, buddy,' I whispered.

Paulo chuckled. 'Oh, Fish-Guts has plan. Fish-Guts going to save the day!'

All the men started laughing.

But just then there came an almighty shout. '*SILÊNCIO!!*'

The men stopped laughing and Fabio leaped down from the tree, not unlike a South American Spider-Man. He turned to Martin and looked him right in the eye.

'You betrayed us, Fish-Guts.'

'I know,' admitted Martin. 'I'm sorry, Fabio.

All of you – I'm sorry. I was led astray by a Game Boy.'

Fabio frowned. 'What is that – some kind of demon?'

'Eh. Sort of . . .'

'Fish-Guts, just tell me this. Can we trust you?'

Martin nodded solemnly.

'Swear it. On your mother's life.'

'Can I swear it on my sisters' lives instead?'

Fabio shrugged. 'OK.'

'Then I swear it. May they all experience terrible hardship and some really annoying stuff if I'm lying. Or if I'm telling the truth, I really don't mind.'

Fabio stepped forward and put a hand on his shoulder. 'I knew you'd come, my friend.'

He then turned to the others and proclaimed, 'What we need is a plan! And this boy has got one! So let's see if Fish-Guts has the guts to get us fish-gutters gutting fish again!!'

CHAPTER TWENTY-SIX
ESCAPE TO FISHY VICTORY

Martin cracked open the back door of the Moone home and we peeped inside. The kitchen was deserted, but we could see his three sisters sprawled on the couch in the living room, watching the *Dynasty Christmas Special*. Martin smiled, knowing they wouldn't be budging any time soon.

He turned to the gang of Brazilians who were crouched at the back door beside him.

'OK, lads, looks like the coast is clear,' he whispered. 'Keep low and quiet. Eyes on me, people.'

He then made several confusing hand gestures that he'd seen in *The A-Team*.

'Tango tango,' he whispered, and crept into the house.

The Brazilians looked
bewildered, but just
shrugged and followed
after him.

They crawled
through the living
room in a long line, like
a silent centipede of
foreign fish-filleters.

We managed to
make it to the hallway
undetected, and could hear
Martin's parents arguing in
their bedroom.

'But, Liam, you were supposed to
do *Christmas* crackers,' complained
Debra. 'These are cheese crackers.'

'They're crackers, aren't they?
And it's Christmas. So they're

Christmas crackers,' retorted Liam.

'But crackers are supposed to have fun stuff inside them, like jokes and party hats.'

'No one's stopping ya wearing these as hats, Deb.'

We quickly slipped inside Martin's bedroom. It was a bit of a squash, but we managed to shut the door.

'Fish-Guts, who this?' whispered Fabio, looking worried.

The men were peering at the round-faced boy who stood in the middle of the room waving at them.

'*Olá, amigos!* Call me P-Dog. I come in peace.'

Martin hurried over. 'Er, this is Padraic. He's going to help us.'

'Indeed I am. And as I understand it, we have little time and much to do. So let's dispense with the pleasantries, shall we, gentlemen?'

Fabio looked to Martin. 'So what's the plan, Fish-Guts?'

'Oh, actually – speaking of pleasantries,

I brought some buns,' interrupted Padraic, opening a tin. 'Who wants one?'

The men all helped themselves to Padraic's buns as Martin pitched his plan.

'My friends, firstly, thank you all for trusting in me – you won't regret it. Secondly, please save me one of those buns. And thirdly, the plan is this. For the past several weeks I have been the victim of a series of attacks. Nocturnal assaults from my three sisters. While I slumbered in my bed, they carefully painted my face to look like a lady. And although this brought me much mockery from my classmates, it also gave me an idea.'

He stopped and faced them all. 'One word: camouflage.'

They looked at him blankly. 'What is . . . camel flags?' asked Fabio, with a mouth full of bun.

'OK, another word – disguise.'

'What is that?'

'OK. Let me try lots of words instead. Right

now, the authorities are searching for thirty Brazilian guys. But you know what they're *not* searching for?' He lifted a sheet from his bed, revealing three make-up kits, with brushes and lipsticks at the ready. 'Thirty Brazilian women!' he declared triumphantly.

'Boom!' I cried. 'You're welcome, Brazilians!'

But the men just stared at Martin, clearly too impressed to applaud.

'Lipstick?' asked Fabio. 'This is your plan, Fish-Guts?'

'Tell them the kicker, buddy,' I urged.

He nodded. 'And here's the cherry on top,' Martin continued. 'Not only will we avoid detection and get you to the factory, but we're also going to use up all my sisters' make-up – so they won't be able to deface me any more, or even hide their own spot-riddled ghost faces!'

'Double boom!' I cried, punching the air twice. 'This plan works on so many levels!'

Fabio frowned. 'Have you really thought this

through, Fish-Guts? Paulo's got a beard.'

Martin chuckled. 'You think he'll be the first bearded lady in Boyle? Not by a long shot, *hombre*.'

'It's going to be brilliant!' chirped Padraic excitedly. 'We're all going to put on make-up and pretend to be women!'

Martin frowned at him. 'But why would you need to do it, Padraic? No one's looking for you.'

'I just want to be part of the gang.'

'I can't just be one guy with thirty-one women,' protested Martin. 'What am I, Magnum, P.I.*?'

Just then, the doorbell rang.

'Hush!' said Paulo. 'Somebody's coming!'

Liam wandered out of his bedroom and answered the door. Then there were muffled

*MAGNUM, P.I. — a moustachioed private investigator on TV. He loved his moustache like he loved his ladies — smooth, silky, and with a faint taste of soup.

voices in the hallway, but we couldn't make out what they were saying. We all stood there, frozen, straining to hear.

'Who's for more buns?' asked Padraic.

'Shush!' Martin hissed.

He cracked open his bedroom door and peeked out.

And there, standing in the hallway, was Bridget Cross!

There were several Gardai* with her too, looking very bored.

'Illegal immigrants were spotted, Mr Moone,' Bridget was telling Liam, 'approaching this very house.'

'Immigrants? In Boyle?' asked Liam. 'Sure who'd immigrate here?'

'Brazilian fishermen, that's who.'

This confused Liam even more. 'Hang on.

*GARDAI — Irish policemen, pronounced 'gardee'. Although, if they're in a car, they're known as 'cardee'. And if they're in the distance, they're 'fardee'.

So you're saying that a bunch of guys left Brazil, the land of rainforests, sunshine and the most beautiful ladies on Earth, and have come here to Boyle in the west of Ireland – to do what exactly?'

'To gut fish, Liam,' replied Garda Pat. 'Isn't it gas? Haha. How are tricks with you anyway? Still playing the handball?'

'Ah, not much any more, Pat. The ol' back is giving me gyp.'

Bridget was losing her patience and shoved a photograph in Liam's face. 'These are the people we're looking for, Mr Moone.'

It was one of Padraic's snaps from the Festival of the Whales, and Liam peered at it.

'Is that Martin . . . doing the samba?'

'I'm afraid so,' replied the Garda. 'In a pub. With illegal immigrants, one of whom was dressed as a whale.'

Liam looked a bit shocked and yelled out, 'Martin!'

Exhibit A

'He's probably in the bathroom,' suggested Bridget. 'He has a very weak bladder.'

Liam marched off to the bathroom and Martin quickly shut his bedroom door.

'We're cornered!' he whispered urgently. 'What are we going to do?'

'Way ahead of ya, Martin,' said Padraic. He was now wearing a lady's dress and was covered in make-up.

'We don't have time for makeovers, Padraic!

We've got to escape! But how?'

I strode over to the window and pointed into the garden. 'That's how, buddy.'

Martin's eyes followed my finger. 'In the wheelbarrow? We'll never fit!'

'The wall, Martin, the wall!'

Realization slowly dawned on his dopey face. 'The wall!! Of course!' he cried.

Three seconds later we were all piling out the window into the back garden. And three seconds after that, we were all charging through the hole in the wall.

At the same time, Liam returned to the others in the hallway.

'No sign of him in the jacks,' he reported. 'I'll check his bedroom now.'

'Right-o, Liam,' called Garda Pat.

Liam knocked on Martin's door. 'Martin? The police are here for ya! Were you off in some pub, dancing with a whale?' he called. 'Martin?'

Sick of waiting, Bridget barged past him and

threw open the door. But the room was empty apart from Padraic, who was wearing a dress and eating a bun. 'Hiya, Auntie!'

Bridget spotted the open window. She pushed past Liam again and came rushing out into the garden, followed by the Gardai and Martin's parents.

'What's going on?' asked Debra.

'They've escaped!' squawked Bridget furiously.

Just then, Debra saw the full destruction of the wall. 'Holy moly,' she gasped. 'Look at that flippin' hole!'

'That's no squirrel damage!' said Liam angrily. 'MARTIN!!!'

But by this stage Martin was in the far corner of the school yard, holding open the metal grate, as the last of the Brazilians dropped into the secret passageway.

'I knew this would come in handy!' he cheered.

We high-fived each other and followed the

Brazilians down. Then we pulled the grate shut
and headed off with the workers, strolling
through the darkness, evading the checkpoint
and singing the Fish-Guts song.

CHAPTER TWENTY-SEVEN
RETURN OF THE KING

We made it to the factory undetected.
Thankfully the Christmas fish were still
nicely iced up, as plump and plucky as a pile
of pregnant plums. The Brazilians got to work
right away and Martin grabbed his bits-brush –
but Fabio stopped him.

'No, Fish-Guts. No sweep-sweep-bang-bang
for you today. We need all the help we can get.
Today you are fish-gutter.'

Martin looked stunned. And honoured. And
worried. And a teeny bit sleepy. 'But . . . these
are the Christmas fish,' he protested, shaking
his head. 'I couldn't possibly—'

'You are ready,' said Fabio firmly, with his
dark, chocolaty eyes fixed on the boy's peanut-
butter-speckled face. (We'd had a very rushed

breakfast.) 'The people of Boyle are depending on us. It is time, Fish-Guts. Today you are little girl no more.'

Martin brightened. 'Oh! That's good!'

'Now you are like big woman.'

Martin gave an uncertain nod. 'Er, OK.'

The men cheered. '*Senhora Fish-Guts!*'

TRANSLATION
Lady Fish-Guts!

I thought they were making fun of him, but they actually saluted him respectfully when they said this, which was even more confusing.

'Wait, do they actually think that's a compliment?' I asked.

But before Martin could reply, Fabio thrust a filleting knife into the boy's hands. 'Gut like the wind, my friend.'

Martin nodded and quickly joined the others at work.

He sliced and sang with his fellow fishermen as they swiftly cleaned the huge fish stock, preparing a beautiful boneless bounty for the hungry bellies of Boyle.

A while later, they were down to the last few fish when suddenly they were interrupted by a loud banging on the factory doors.

The workers froze mid-song, apart from Bill who kept on warbling away happily. Brendan blindly cupped a hand over his friend's mouth (it was actually his nose, but Bill got the idea).

THUMP-THUMP-THUMP! went the doors again.

'*Oscail an doras!*' hollered Bridget. 'We know you're in there!'

TRANSLATION
Open the door!

'How did they find us?' I whispered to Martin.

As if to answer me, Bridget yelled, 'We could hear ye singing!'

'Oh balls,' moaned Martin. 'What are we gonna do?'

Just then we heard a familiar 'Mmeeaauurggghgh!'

We looked down to see Fishsticks at our feet. And a moment later we were hit by a powerful stench.

'Mr Feeley!' Martin gasped, partly in shock and partly because of the pong.

'The fish king is back!' announced Francie, looking even greasier than usual, standing before us in a fishnet vest*.

'You here to save us, Senhor Feeley?' asked Paulo.

'Actually, no, Paulo, I just popped out because I was dyin' for some nice—'

Francie's eyes then fell on the pile of filleted Christmas fish, and he paused. He stepped forward slowly, marvelling at their beautiful boneless bodies.

'Good God,' he murmured, 'they're perfect . . .'

'Thank you, senhor,' said Fabio.

THUMP-THUMP-THUMP!

The noise startled Francie and he looked at

---

* **FISHNET VEST** — a vest with lots of holes in it. Very handy if you unexpectedly need to net a fish, or catch a butterfly, or strain some pasta.

the workers, suddenly concerned. 'Go, Fabio. Paulo. All of you. Go.'

'Go where?'

'Use my secret hiding place.'

'But . . . we'll never fit.'

'It's actually roomier than it looks,' Francie told him. 'There's fifty of my finest paintings in there. Chuck them out, and that should do it.'

'Chuck them out?'

Francie was still looking at the fish with deep admiration. 'It's you who are the real artists. I see that now,' he whispered. 'Now go!'

Fabio turned, but Francie pulled him back. 'Wait! C'mere and give us a hug, ya big bronzed beauty.'

He squeezed Fabio tight.

'Now go, I said!' he yelled, suddenly releasing him.

The Brazilians sprang into action, each grabbing an armful of the Christmas fish. They hurried away, desperate to get themselves and the fish out of sight, and even more desperate to avoid a hug from Francie. They rushed up the narrow staircase towards the office.

A moment later, a loud *BOOM* reverberated around the factory.

'What the flip? They're breaking down the door!' I yelled to Martin.

The workers were still scampering upstairs. Brendan tripped over Fishsticks and several of the men went tumbling over each other, dropping the precious fish.

BOOM went the door again, and this time it strained on its hinges.

Francie looked worried now.

'They're never gonna make it, buddy!' I cried.

Martin called to Francie, looking desperate. 'They need more time, Mr Feeley, sir!'

Francie nodded. And with a determined look he marched over to the factory doors. He threw them open, facing the angry mob head on.

'Stop this madness!' he cried. 'I'm the one you want, not them. Them who aren't even here. But me who is. Francie Feeley!'

Bridget stood there with her posse* of police and other folks who were against the workers.

They looked startled by Francie's arrival, and he stood tall, with fire in his belly, strength in his heart and tuna fish on his lips.

'I confess it all!' he continued. 'I'm the one who nabbed them from their starving village and brought them here on my yacht. Why did I do it? Because my yacht was broken and I needed thirty strong men to row me back to Ireland? Probably. To be honest, I can't remember – I was very sunburned at the time. But I took care of those lads like they were my own spawn. I let them eat all the fish they could catch and sing all the depressing songs they wanted. Did I let them use my jet ski? Of course not. Every time they asked, I told them it was broken. Was that wrong? Probably. But I'm no hero, people. I'm just a man who loves fish.'

He paused, glancing to his side, and could see

*POSSE — a gang. It's pronounced possey, but there's no Y because the other letters all formed an angry posse and chased it away.

that the workers were still struggling to get out
of sight, scrambling up the stairs, climbing over
Brendan who was still wrestling with Fishsticks.

'And that's why I brought them here and put them to work,' continued Francie. 'Did I pay them less than my cat? Yes, I did. Did I make them sleep four to a bed in the cheapest pub in Just Outside Boyle? Absolutely. Is that a crime? Is it a crime to create jobs? Is it a crime to hug everyone you see and put a smile on their face? Is it a crime to use fish-guts as the main ingredient of sherbet and sell it to unsuspecting children all around the country? Probably. But it's too late now because I've used fish-guts in more products than you could ever imagine. I've turned it into powder, jellies, glues, paint, onion rings, toothpaste, face cream, chicken nuggets, microwaveable popcorn –'

Upstairs, the workers were frantically hauling out the paintings and cramming themselves inside the secret chamber.

'Hurry, lads, hurry!' urged Martin.

Below them, Francie continued: 'It's the most versatile substance known to man! Name any product. Dolls' eyes: 56% fish-guts. Cake sprinkles: 93% fish-guts. Tennis-racket grips. Ever wondered why they sometimes get sticky? Two words, my friends. Mackerel livers. Magic birthday candles. Why do they keep relighting? Eel hearts, that's why. What makes chewing gum so stretchy? Shark stomachs.'

Finally, when the lads were out of sight, Martin raced back downstairs. He gave a thumbs-up to Francie, who gave a nod and wrapped up his speech.

'So, in conclusion, all I did was save a village and give some young fishermen a taste of freedom by sneaking them into the country and forcing them to gut fish. And if that's a crime, then you might as well just lock me up and throw away the key!'

The Gardai and Bridget looked at each other.

Francie gave a satisfied smile, confident that his noble words had swayed their opinions of him.

'Right, lads, lock him up,' said Garda Pat.

'Oh balls,' muttered Francie, as they clamped a pair of handcuffs on him.

But before they could haul him away, Martin ran over to him.

'Mr Feeley, sir, thank you!' He then whispered, 'But why did you come out? You could have just stayed hidden.'

Francie smiled. 'Martin, when we first met, I told you that there were two things you needed to know about me. The first was that I love fish. Well, the second thing is this: I also love chips. And after eating all that tinned fish I was dyin' for some nice chips.' He turned to Garda Pat. 'Garda, can we stop at the chipper on the way to jail?'

Pat shrugged. 'I don't see why not.'

'Lovely stuff,' said Francie.

And with that, they led him away.

Bridget barged past him and peered around the empty factory.

'They're here somewhere,' she growled. 'Find them!'

CHAPTER TWENTY-EIGHT
'TWAS THE NIGHT
BEFORE CHRISTMAS

Bridget's mob moved in and began to search the factory. And among the Brazilian-begrudgers, I suddenly spotted a familiar face.

'Whoa! What's Mr Jackson doing here?' I whispered to Martin.

We hadn't seen his teacher since Martin had made his big, fiery speech about freedom and potatoes.

'Aw no,' he gulped. 'Hide!'

He grabbed a big coat that was hanging nearby and threw it over us like a tent.

'Good thinking, buddy,' I told him. 'If he can't see you, then he can't expel you.'

'You think he's going to expel me?!'

'Not now, he won't! All we have to do is stay under this coat forever.'

Martin peeped out through one of the
sleeves. His teacher was standing near Bridget,
who had clearly taken over the operation and
was barking orders at everyone.

'You, search the fish truck. You lads, secure
the perimeter. Jackson, check Feeley's office.'

Mr Jackson nodded and moved towards the
office, where all the workers were hiding.

'Oh balls . . .' we murmured.

A few minutes later, the sleeve of our large coat
peeped through the office door. We could see
Mr Jackson searching the room.

'Don't worry, buddy, he'll never find the
secret hiding place,' I whispered. 'I mean, it took
us *ages* to—'

'He's found it!' yelped Martin.

And sure enough, Mr Jackson was now
peering at the little hinge beside the painting!

In a last-ditch effort to save his pals, Martin
suddenly threw off the coat and burst into
the room.

'Hey there, Mr Jackson!'

His teacher swivelled round, startled. 'Moone! What do you want?' he grunted. 'You here to have another spuds rant?'

'Hahahahahaha!' laughed Martin, for a bit too long. 'Spuds? I'd forgotten all about that. No, no, I just came here to . . . to say Merry Christmas . . . Eve.'

Jackson frowned. 'Merry Christmas Eve?'

'That doesn't sound right, does it? What do you say on Christmas Eve? Happy The-Day-Before-Christmas?'

'You don't say anything, Moone.'

'Hahahaha! Good old Mr Jackson,' Martin laughed, and patted his teacher on the arm. 'Well, this room looks empty! Shall we check the break room now? Could've sworn I saw a few Brazilians hanging out near the Skiffles machine earlier.'

Twang!

Mr Jackson's head snapped round, hearing the faint musical hiccup that came from behind the painting. 'What was that?' he asked.

Martin and I shared a worried look. We both knew that it was Fabio's guitar – someone must have brushed against it.

'That was . . . me sneezing!' said Martin. 'I have a very musical sneeze.'

'But you didn't sneeze, Moone.'

'Did I not? That's weird. Oh well. Want to see where I keep my fish-gut brushes?'

But Mr Jackson was peering at the painting again. He grasped one side of it and suddenly pulled it open like a door. And there before him were the thirty fish-gutters, crammed into the secret space like sardines.

There was a pause as Mr Jackson took in the sight.

Martin and I gulped.

We could hear Bridget approaching, and our hearts sank, knowing that our friends were doomed.

But then his teacher did something unexpected – he took hold of the painting and closed it again.

Martin and I looked at each other, confused. We were so thrown that we almost forgot to hide. But at the last moment we leaped behind the Bee-Gees jukebox just before Bridget walked in.

'Any sign of them, Jackson?' she asked.

He shook his head. 'Nah. Just a bunch of pictures of Mr Feeley riding dolphins,' he said, gesturing at a pile of paintings nearby.

Bridget sighed in frustration. 'Well, keep looking. They've got to be here somewhere.'

She glanced at her watch. 'I need to get back to the butcher shop. Something tells me that business is about to start really picking up . . .' she said with a smirk.

Then she walked off, treading on one of Francie's paintings as she went.

When she was gone, we popped out from behind the jukebox.

'You saved them, sir!' said Martin in amazement.

His teacher shrugged. 'I suppose I did,' he grunted. 'Hadn't really planned it like that, to be honest. But I've been thinking about your little outburst, Moone,' he said. 'Maybe you're right. Maybe we shouldn't just eat spuds. And maybe they don't need that ol' Berlin Wall. And maybe cats and dogs *should* marry.'

'Not sure we're really behind that one,' I murmured to Martin.

'I must say, it's rare that a pupil teaches you anything,' continued Mr Jackson. 'Extremely rare. To be honest, the last people in the world that I'd expect to teach me something are you shower of dopey little dimwits. I thought I'd be more likely to learn something from a freshly pooped cowpat in a field than from you stupid muppets.'

He put a hand on Martin's shoulder. 'But you changed my mind, Martin. And you only need to change one person's mind to make a difference.

'I read that in a Christmas cracker once,' he added. 'There's more than hats and jokes inside them, you know. There's wise sayings too. And sometimes even a whistle or something.'

He patted Martin on the head and went to leave.

'Merry Christmas Eve, Martin,' he said with a wink, and walked away.

I looked at Martin. 'Did he just call us muppets?'

When Bridget arrived at Cross Country Meats, she saw a large crowd outside the Fishatorium. And for the first time ever, this pleased her very much. Francie's customers had come to collect the Christmas fish they'd ordered, but there was no sign of Francie.

'Hello?' called Debra Moone, as she knocked on the door. 'Anyone in there?'

'He's not coming!' cried Gerry Bonner, starting to panic. 'We've been shafted, Debra! I knew I shouldn't have paid for those fishes upfront! Why am I always so bloody trusting?!'

'Calm down, Gerry. He's probably just running late.'

'Don't tell me to calm down!' he snapped. 'What are we going to eat for Christmas dinner? Just a whole load of vegetables? Jonner and Conor won't stand for it. They'll slash my tyres again. Just like they did last year when I forgot the cranberry sauce*!'

'I'm sure Mr Feeley will be here any minute.'

'Oh, I wouldn't count on it, Mrs Moone!' called Bridget. 'I'm afraid fish might be off the menu this year!'

They all turned to her, looking alarmed.

*CRANBERRY SAUCE — ham jam.

'But never fear,' Bridget reassured them, 'I've got plenty of tasty meats to go around.'

'Oh thank flip,' sighed Gerry.

'However,' added Bridget, 'I've decided to raise my prices. I'll be charging five times the usual amount.'

'Five times?!' gasped Gerry.

'We're not paying that!' yelled Debra. 'You can't hold this town to ransom!'

Bridget chuckled. 'Oh, can't I, Debra?'

She looked at her watch. 'I make it just after 6 p.m. on Christmas Eve. Your shopping options are very limited – unless you want broccoli sandwiches for your Christmas dinner?'

'Good God, no,' murmured Gerry.

A meat delivery truck pulled up nearby and started to unload more turkeys for Bridget – she was clearly stocking up.

'I'll be open tomorrow morning at 9 a.m.,' she announced to the crowd, 'the only place open on Christmas Day. And by then,' she said, with a malevolent grin, 'I bet you'll all be begging me to sell you a turkey!'

She cackled with laughter and sauntered into her shop.

*

'Twas the night before Christmas,
When all through the factory,
Not a creature was stirring,
Except a boy on a tractor-y.

It was Padraic! After the police had left empty-handed, he rolled up in his dad's Massey Ferguson*, eager to help.

'P-Dog!' cried Martin, and the two pals high-fived.

The boys joined the others, who were gathered together on the factory floor – Declan Mannion, Bill and Brendan, and the Brazilian fish-gutters. They nodded at Padraic and pretended not to notice that he was still wearing a dress.

*MASSEY FERGUSON — the Rolls-Royce of tractors (if a Rolls-Royce drove at four miles an hour, stank of manure, and was constantly being chased by a dog).

'So what's the plan, Fish-Guts?' asked Fabio.

'Well, we may not have been able to get the fish to the Fishatorium for collection,' Martin admitted, 'but we can still get a Christmas fish to everyone who ordered one.'

Declan held up a sheet of paper. 'I've got the list of customers.'

'He's making a list, and checking it twice,' sang Padraic with a chuckle.

'No, I just checked it once,' said Declan blankly.

Padraic nodded. 'Okey-doke. That's probably enough.'

We found several large sacks in the sack room and divided the fish between them. Then our Father Fishmases hoisted them over their shoulders.

They clambered on to Padraic's dad's tractor, and Martin and I ran in front to make sure the coast was clear. Like a couple of reindeer, we guided them through the sleeping town as they delivered the fish to everyone's door, stuffing them through their letter boxes.

And Martin yelled out,
Giving us all a good fright,
'Happy Christmas to all,
And to all a good night!'

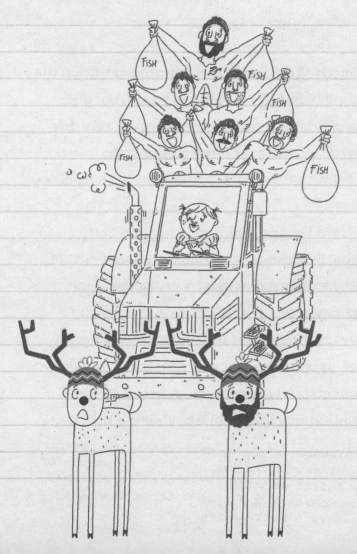

CHAPTER TWENTY-NINE
ZERO SLEEPS TO CHRISTMAS

Surely there is no greater festive tradition than
a giddy family skipping to their front door
on Christmas morning to discover a freshly
wrapped haddock lying on the mat.

Oh, that's not a tradition in your house, you
say?!

Well, you're really missing out. I pity
you. Because as the excited boys and girls of
Boyle rushed downstairs to discover their
pongy present, a collective gasp could be
heard throughout the county. It was a gasp
of joy, surprise, but also confusion. You can
understand the concern. A fish through
the letter box feels like a symbol* for

*SYMBOL — a thing that really represents
another thing. For example, a symbol for
a toilet is usually an outline of a man
or woman, and a symbol for a drum kit is
always a cymbal.

something. But for what exactly?

'Simon, I'm confused . . .' a local girl lisped to her big brother as she held the fish aloft. 'I knows if we've been nice all year, we gets presents, and if we've been naughty, we gets lumps of coal, but what does a fish gift mean?'

'I think it means . . .' the equally perplexed little man replied, 'I think it means we've been smelly all year?'

The children's confusion was matched only by their parents' delight. On finding that Christmas lunch was back on, mams and dads all over town called out in collective merriment –

'Thank you, Francie Feeley!'

'Damn you, Francie Feeley!' was the response by only one greedy grinch.

Bridget Cross was standing alone in the middle of her bursting butcher shop. But to her shock, her store wasn't brimming with desperate customers, but rather with dozens and dozens of plump, overpriced turkeys.

As her furious gaze fell from her overflowing

shop window to her dirty doormat, she spotted a present of her own.

When she picked up the stinky sea meat, she noticed a hand-scribbled note had been attached –

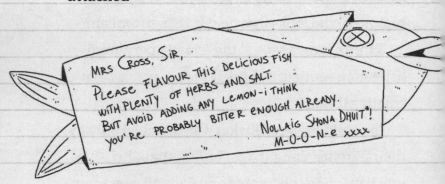

Mrs Cross, Sir,
Please FLAVOUR THIS DELICIOUS FISH WITH PLENTY OF HERBS AND SALT. BUT AVOID ADDING ANY LEMON - I THINK YOU'RE PROBABLY BITTER ENOUGH ALREADY.
NOLLAIG SHONA DHUIT*!
M-O-O-N-e xxxx

Even though the day's terrible turn of events had left her seething, Bridget couldn't help but grin at Martin's correct use of Irish.

'Chirpy flippin *amadán*,' she smiled to herself, as she punched a tubby turkey in frustration.

*NOLLAIG SHONA DHUIT — Irish for Merry Christmas to you. The Irish word for Christmas is Nollaig. Which is why in Ireland, Father Christmas is called Noel. Dr Noel Christmas.

*

Meanwhile in the Moone house, the *amadán*
in question was just awakening from his well-
earned slumber. His nocturnal dispatches
had left the little fella pretty zonked. This was
definitely the first time he'd had to be woken
up on a Christmas morning. Usually by 5 a.m.
he'd be ripping through wrapping and chucking
down chocolate, but it was 10.37 before Martin's
parents finally stood cheerily over his bed.

'Merry Christmas, sleepyhead!' Debra
proclaimed, as she handed him a beribboned
gift with a wry smile.

'Holy moly, buddy!' I said, only just waking
up myself. 'Is it Christmas?! Did I sleep
through it? Is that your present? What is it?
Am I asking too many questions?'

'As you know . . .' Liam began cautiously, 'the
Moone family money mountain isn't very tall
this year, Martin.'

'It's more like a moolah molehill,' Debra
muttered under her breath.

'But we knew what you were after, so . . .
I did everything in my power to deliver it.'

'Thanks, Daddy-o,' Martin said excitedly.

Without further ado, Martin ripped
into the present like a ThunderCat, leaving
Debra to gather up the strewn wrapping
paper.

(She would always do this with the intention
of keeping it for next year. It would then sit in a
box for a few weeks before being thrown on the
fire during a cold snap in March.)

As he pulled back the wrapping paper
we could see the bottom half of the box. It
read: 'me boy'! We shared an elated glance of
anticipation.

'Now, I'm no librarian, buddy,' I started
excitedly, 'but I'm pretty sure those are the
last five letters of GAME BOY!!!'

'I know!' he squeaked.

'You know *what*, Martin?' Liam asked, but
their little man was too engrossed to listen.

'I think they've done it!' I yelped. 'They've

only gone and flippin' done it like a pair of legends!!!!'

As he ripped asunder the remaining wrapping, we began to realize that our excitement was somewhat premature. The packaging had a cereal-box quality, the lettering looked hand-drawn, and as the last of the paper fell to the floor, we saw that written on it were the words 'SAME BOY'.

'It's not quite the Game Boy ya wanted, pal, but . . . it's kinda the same, no?'

It turned out that Liam had tried to make a Game Boy himself in his workshop! He'd brought in a couple of lads to help him of course. They'd taken parts from unused radios, discarded buttons from a table lamp and the digital display from a broken microwave. All to create this Frankenstein's monster of hand-held computing.

'Yeah, Dad, totally the same,' he lied, rather sweetly. 'Thanks a million.'

Liam nodded happily and headed off to look

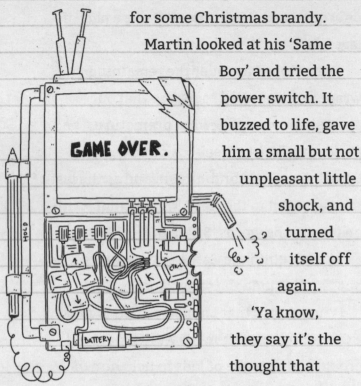

for some Christmas brandy. Martin looked at his 'Same Boy' and tried the power switch. It buzzed to life, gave him a small but not unpleasant little shock, and turned itself off again.

'Ya know, they say it's the thought that counts,' I said wisely, 'but when your dad had this idea, he really should have counted his thoughts.'

Martin shook his head and had another go on his new electrocution machine.

'Listen, Martin,' asked Debra, still collecting useless paper, 'I have to ask, how did you do it?'

'Well, Mam, I just turned it on, and it shocked the flip outta me!'

'What? No, Martin, I mean the tree in the garden. How did you get it?'

We shared a baffled look, hopped up and headed for the garden.

As we passed through the sitting room, we found Fidelma, Trisha and Sinead with ghostly white faces. They were all wearing the face cream Martin had got them for Christmas.

'Eh, this stuff is actually . . . kinda cool. So, like, thanks,' Trisha muttered.

'No bother, ladies. I know how much you girls love your faces.'

He thought it best not to mention the actual contents of 'Francie Feeley's Fabulous Face Cream' and continued his journey to the garden.

Debra wasn't joking – there was a massive Christmas tree right slap bang behind the

Moone house. It seemed to have grown there overnight.

I had a thought. 'Buddy, do ya think maybe those magic beans that we bought off Declan Mannion finally sprouted?'

But then Martin suddenly remembered something and checked his pocket. It was empty. 'The fir cone!' he exclaimed. 'It must have fallen out of my pocket when we came in last night!'

'Hippy Christmash, Martin!'

We looked over to see Bruce the Spruce waving from the end of the garden.

'Thanks, Bruce!' called Martin. 'You too!'

The huge tree then climbed awkwardly into the field next door.

'Climbing a tree isn't half as much fun as watching a tree climb,' I noted.

'Good old Bruce,' Martin said. 'I knew he'd come through in the end.'

'Who'd come through?' Liam asked, appearing from the back door.

'Oh. Ya know . . .' Martin stumbled, 'you. With the whole Same Boy thing.'

Liam nodded in agreement, clearly happy with his handiwork.

'Well, I *am* a whizz with machines,' he smugly announced.

'So we got a last-minute tree, our festive fish in the post – how can this day get any better?' Debra marvelled.

'I know the answer to that!' Martin chirped.

Then the doorbell rang. Liam and Debra shared a confused look. They clearly weren't expecting visitors.

'I invited thirty Brazilians over for Christmas lunch.'

CHAPTER THIRTY
PLENTY OF ROOM AT THE INN

As the swarm of South Americans spilt through the door, Martin was taken aback by his parents' reaction. He'd expected some harsh looks or words or even slaps to be thrown in his direction. But no, they just hurried about the kitchen, readying every pot and pan in the house for their new guests.

'Are ye not going to . . . shout at me or something?' Martin asked honestly.

'What? Why would we do that?' Debra replied, scrubbing a grimy pot.

'Well, for inviting all these strangers over for lunch?'

'Isn't it Christmas Day, Martin?'

'Yeah . . . ?' Martin shrugged.

Liam shared a look with Debra and

pointed into the sitting room.

'Ya see that candle in the window? Why do you think that's there?'

'To replace the lamp you destroyed to assemble my Lame Boy?'

'*Same Boy*,' Liam corrected him.

'Sorry, yes, my Same Boy.'

'No, Martin, that candle means, at Christmas, our house is open to anyone who needs a home. That's what Christmas is about. Everything else is just advertising.'

Martin didn't really understand what that meant, but he was happy they were happy. And he was delighted the Brazilians had joined them for the day. And he was slightly worried the candle in the window might set the curtains on fire. But just then Fabio emerged from the sitting room and approached the Moones with a typical flick of his silky locks.

'Oh, Fish-Guts,' Fabio said, gently taking Debra's hand, 'this must be your sister.'

'Hehehahhahahahhehe!' Debra giggled like a

woman half her age. Who had just fallen over. And was embarrassed by people seeing her slip. And was maybe an idiot.

'What? No! No, haha. No, I'm Martin's mother actually. Haha.'

'Who is Martin?'

'Hahaha. You . . . must be Fab . . . I mean . . . Fabio . . . hahah . . . His sister! . . . Hahaha.'

She laughed like a maniac for quite a while. She giggled for so long, in fact, that Fabio eventually just wandered off and started talking to someone else.

As the day went on, more and more people arrived. Padraic and Trevor stopped in with cakes and leftover crackers. Bill and Brendan swung by, got lost in the hallway and left again. Mr Jackson brought his fancy new Polaroid camera to have pictures taken with the Brazilians. Linda and the ladies from Just Outside Boyle came by to giggle too loudly with Debra. Even Fishsticks showed up.

Sinead chased him around for a while. Then there was scratching and some crying. But I didn't see which came from which catty creature.

And Christmas lunch was a storming success. It turned out the Brazilians didn't just know how to *gut* fish. They could cook like the wind too. It was quite the exotic fishy feat. And not a single Brussels sprout in sight. By the day's end, half the town was there. The music soared, the port* was poured and the 'OK Christmas' was turning into the Best Christmas Ever.

As tropical music played in the chilly Moone back garden, myself and Crunchie Haystacks played imaginary tag around the giant Christmas tree. While we frolicked, Padraic and Martin had a chinwag about the events of the day.

*PORT — a dessert wine from Portugal. I would imagine any drink would be welcome if you were stuck in a dessert like the Kalahari or the Sahara.

'So, what did you get for Christmas, Martin?'

'I got . . . Well, it's . . .' Martin stuttered, a little embarrassed. 'My dad made me something.'

'Cool. My dad still gets my name wrong sometimes,' Padraic replied.

'Really? What does he call you?'

'Peter. I've corrected him, of course I have, but after a while I just gave up and now I just answer to Peter.'

'That's kind of weird.'

'It's completely weird, Martin, but that's the lot I got.'

'Well, I suppose you didn't really need presents, what with your fancy new Game Boy and everything.'

'What? No, I gave that thing away.'

'What?!' Martin barked. 'To who?!'

'Oh . . . just a friend.'

'A friend who's not me? What were ya thinking, P? Why didn't you—'

But Martin's rant was interrupted by

some cheering from the house.

'Declano!' came a chant from inside. 'Declano the Volcano!'

Martin and Padraic rushed in to find that Declan Mannion had arrived and was being hugged vigorously by the Brazilians. They seemed delighted to see him for some reason.

'All right, lads, all right. Don't crease the denim,' he insisted, patting down his blue jacket and jeans.

'What's going on, Fabio?' Martin asked, as his foreign friend ruffled Declan's hair and the boys lifted him on to their shoulders.

'Declano has our Christmas bonuses, Fish-Guts!'

'That's right, lads,' Declan agreed, as he handed each man a packed envelope. 'Don't spend it all at once. Unless you're buying a house or a car or whatever.'

'You got the money from Francie?' Martin asked, surprised.

'Yeah, I've just come from the prison now.

He's happy as Larry* up there. When I left him, he was putting the finishing touches to a mural he'd painted on his cell wall of himself fighting an octopus. It was pretty good. Nice shadow detail. The man has a talent.'

'Well, Fish-Guts. You know what that means . . .' said Fabio.

'Francie's going to become a painter?' Martin shrugged.

'No, buddy,' I whispered. 'I think it means they're going home.'

'What? You can't go back to Brazil. Everyone wants you here now.'

Fabio put his hand on Martin's shoulder and smiled warmly.

'Everyone except our families.'

Martin nodded. After today, he understood how important being with family was. It was going to be hard to go back to a life without

*HAPPY AS LARRY — this expression refers to Larry Stapleton. He was well known as a happy person. Nothing else is known about him.

his new friends, but who knew what surprises tomorrow's yection would bring. Well, I did, but I wanted it to be a surprise, so I kept quiet.

'Thank you. Thank you for everything, Fish-Guts.'

'Martin,' Padraic corrected him with a whisper, leaning in.

'And thank you, Martin,' Fabio said to Padraic, not understanding him.

'And thank you again, Declan, for lending us Mr Feeley's yacht.'

Declan shrugged. 'No problemo, Fabio.'

'C'mon, guys, we've got a lot of rowing to do.'

As the Brazilians filed out, excited about getting back to their village, they each stopped to salute their fish-gutting comrade. Martin saluted them in turn. Which eventually made his elbow quite sleepy. There were loads of them.

Finally it was Fabio's turn. He stood at the Moone front door facing Martin. But he didn't salute. He just gave a little wink, a swish of his hair, and he was gone.

In the background, Debra giggled again.

Liam entered and shook his head at his suddenly teenage wife.

'There's a man on the phone. Says he's looking for someone called Peter?'

'That's me,' Padraic grumbled as he headed off home.

'Well, buddy,' I said, trying to lift Martin's spirits, 'Looks like it's just you and me again.'

'Yeah, Sean. That'll do. That'll do just fine.'

'Oh!' I said, spotting one more wrapped gift sitting by the front door. 'I think someone forgot to open that.'

It had his name on it. Well, actually it said 'Fish-Guts'. Martin rushed over and started pulling away the paper eagerly.

A wave of Christmas spirit washed over the boy as he revealed the beautiful fish-shaped guitar. Fabio had left him his most prized possession.

Martin held the guitar close to his chest. It meant a lot that Fabio had given him something so precious. But secretly we both knew he'd always be a little too lazy to learn how to play it. We shared a smile.

'What a lovely ornament,' we said together.

FROM BRAZIL

ALDEIA
DE LAGRIMAS
E PEIXES
MORTOS

ear Fish-Guts!
eetings From Brazil.
day I heard a sweet hummingbird
t hit with a falling stone From cliff.
e sad screeching sound it make on way
death remind me of my little Irish Friend.
o I thought I say hi. Hi.
miss you. We all talk of the day the
lly little boy From Ireland stood
ll For his Foreign Friends. You will
ever be welcome in Brazil. We will
ng songs and eat Food and make jokes
bout how pale you are.
weep-sweep-bang-bang, my marvellous man. Fx

S Please say thank you to your chubby
ittle Friend For his present of Game Boy.
t was very nice him. I gave it to the
retty girl in my village. She thought it was
Fancy new trap For to catch Fish.
o . . . she threw it in sea. Paz e Amor Fabio

FISH-GUTS MOONE,

BOYLE ROAD, BOYLE, CO.

ROSCOMMON, IRELAND

THE END

ABOUT
CHRIS O'DOWD

Chris O'Dowd is an award-winning actor and writer from the barmy town of Boyle in Ireland. Chris did some good acting in *Bridesmaids*, *The IT Crowd*, *Gulliver's Travels* and *Of Mice and Men*. We won't mention the films where he did bad acting. He has a dog called Potato and a cat who shouts at him for no reason. He studied at University College Dublin and the London Academy of Music and Dramatic Art. He graduated from neither. Chris created *Moone Boy* to get revenge on his sisters for putting make-up on him as a child. He co-wrote the Sky TV series and this book with his good friend Nick Murphy, who is a lot older than Chris.

ABOUT
NICK V. MURPHY

Nick V. Murphy is a writer from Kilkenny, Ireland. (The V. in his name stands for Very.) He went to Trinity College Dublin to study English and History, but spent most of his time doing theatre and running away from girls. This was where he bumped into Chris O'Dowd, who was out looking for pizza. After college, Nick focused on writing, which was the laziest career he could think of, as it could even be done while wearing pyjamas. He wrote a few things for TV, then a movie called *Hideaways*, before co-writing a short film with Chris called *Capturing Santa*. The pyjama-wearing pair developed this into the comedy series *Moone Boy*, which recently won an International Emmy for Best Comedy.

THE MARVELLOUS WORLD OF
MOONE BOY

INCLUDES ACTIVITIES, GAMES, JOKES AND CARTOONS!

Spend a day in the life of Martin Moone with this amazing Moone Boy activity book.

Including a brand-new Moone Boy story and loads of puzzles, games, activities and things to make and do, you might just find your very own Imaginary Friend at the end of it all . . .

COMING SOON!

'HARD TO PUT DOWN'
THE BOOKBAG

'WE LOVE THIS
TIMELY STORY'
ANGELS AND URCHINS

'TOTALLY NUTTY, AND
VERY, VERY FUNNY'
LOVEREADING4KIDS

'RAUCOUSLY FUNNY'
IRISH TIMES

'UNIQUE AND
HILARIOUS'
SIDNEY, AGE 11

'I HOPE THIS IS
NOT THE LAST I
HAVE HEARD OF
MARTIN MOONE
AND SEAN MURPHY'
CAMERON, AGE 10

REVIEWS

'HILARIOUS AND BRILLIANT'
FRANK COTTRELL BOYCE

WINNER:
BORD GÁIS
IRISH
CHILDREN'S
BOOK AWARD

'LAUGH-OUT-LOUD'
PRIMARY TIMES IRELAND

'A REAL HOOT, AND PERFECT FOR FANS OF
DAVID WALLIAMS AND DIARY OF A WIMPY KID'
WRD MAGAZINE

'HIGHLY ORIGINAL,
QUIRKY, FUNNY,
HUGELY ENJOYABLE!'
BOOKS MONTHLY

'WILDLY ENTERTAINING . . . IF YOU
MISS OUT ON STRAIGHT-UP CRAIC
LIKE THIS, YOU ARE A GOMBEEN
OF THE HIGHEST ORDER'
THE NEW YORK TIMES

'FULL OF GENTLE
HUMOUR' WE
LOVE THIS BOOK

'A TOTAL BALL!
A LAUGH EVERY PAGE!'
EDWARD, AGE 10

'A BRILLIANTLY FUNNY READ FULL
OF CRAZY CHARACTERS, HILARIOUS
DEFINITIONS AND COOL CARTOONS.
I LOVED IT!' SAM, AGE 11